Tobias

Tobias

Bilbo Books Publishing

www.BilboBooks.com

bilbobookspublishing@gmail.com

ISBN- 978-1-7364598-1-2

Printed in the United States of America

Bilbo Books Publishing. Athens, Georgia

"It is the predisposition of human nature to consider an unpleasant idea untrue."

– Dr. Sigmund Freud

Cascading pictures turn to mist behind my eyes.
Only one retains shape and sets itself apart.

Tobit.

Tobias.

Tobi.

I imagine space. Time ripples over planets and
stars, like a sheet covering us in darkness
as our small planet spins underneath. The
beginning and the end constantly intersect.
East becomes west, as the sun rises and sets.
The start fades to the end and begins again,
making neither exist.

Blink.

I am here again, the thick smell of black
mold clogging each breath. The brown ceiling
crumbles over my perspiring skin. Glossy green
paint stained from leaking pipes and body
fluids curls as the walls crack for a sinking
foundation. I scratch the veneered surface
of a warped tabletop wondering why I left my
meditation so soon.

He is here, body prostrate upon the floor.
Blood dripping from the hole in his head sinks
through the porous wood, bringing life to the
dead, it makes the walls breathe an incessant
breath.

Blink.

"Look at the stars. The city seems darker
tonight." I say with a shuddering breath.

Tobias lights a cigarette with a deep residing
drag. The smoke settles like a fog between
us. He turns slowly to the open window as the
smoke follows like an evil companion. His eyes
keep with mine until I am lost from them. He
leans against the windowsill and a sliver of
moonlight settles on his face.

"You still don't understand. You just won't
see the truth, and now I know it's too late.
I'm sorry, old friend." Tobias breathes out the
words, and the smoke pouring from his mouth
catches the breeze from the window and escapes
into the city.

My left hand is cramping.

My whole body shakes.

The steel is too heavy.

I am too weak.

Blink.

Death.

Blink.

Life.

Blink.

There is no beginning, there is no end. There
is only what remains and what has not survived.
The start fades to the end and begins again,
making neither exist.

It's me.

I'm the fraud.

I'm the killer.

Everything you read from this point on is all at once present and past. Every line is truth and fiction. Each word is who I am and how I see the events that take place. But you must know that who I am changes with the breeze. You will begin to understand who I am and how I think. You will want to judge me whether for the good or the bad and in one sentence you will feel like I have changed entirely, and you will need to start from scratch. I can't be sorry about this because I don't care about you. I don't need you to care for me. These things just have to be said. They always have to be said. When new people come in, I must at least warn them of what's coming.

I won't drag you along for 200 pages thinking that someone else is at fault. This isn't a mystery novel and I'm not the guy who learns any lessons. I'm also no writer. If you are an avid reader, I assure you that it is no

intention of mine to break the rules or "do
my own thing" as it were. In other words,
the mistakes you find are not intentional and
are entirely due to ignorance or more likely,
stupidity.

Sorry.

I don't have that kind of time.

I don't have the patience to sit here and think
of ways to string you along or mislead you.
I'm not trying to be interesting or to sell
a million copies and be featured on the New
York Times Bestsellers list. I'm not trying to
sit next to any one of the dozens of talk show
hosts and explain my brilliant writing method
and how my book is actually a metaphor for
society or some other bullshit.

I have no method.

Like you, I only have my choices, a kind of
actuated method maybe, that lead to other
choices and those choices lead me to several
moments in which I found myself killing those I
loved.

I've heard men say:

"It just happened." Them, cheating on their wives.

"It just happened." Them, beating their children.

"It just happened." Them, getting so wasted they rape their step-kid.

The truth is that the one who cheated on his wife made the decision when he chose to get in his car and go to the bar. The truth is that the one that beat his child made the decision when he chose to never dedicate himself to refraining from impulse. The truth is that the one who raped his step-kid made the decision when he stopped by the store and picked up the twelve pack of whatever cheap shit he wanted to drink.

What I'm saying is that every moment you feel as though one decision has taken your life away, remember that you have been making bad choices a long time to get yourself to this moment.

Don't fool yourself.

Fuck, I'm going on again and I don't have that kind of time. Not here, behind or ahead. The sun will rise, and my moments will be gone.

Just remember, you have been a piece of shit for years and suddenly you blink and you're killing your friends.

Blink.

"Pleshdondoudeesh"

When you have your hands around someone's throat it's hard to understand what they're saying. They slur every word together. Spit goes everywhere.

This is Eddy. He's the guy you can call when you need to talk. He's the guy that makes you feel good about your shit life because his shit life is shittier than yours.

He is my friend.

He is about to die.

He's not the first, but I don't see time as

linear. My brain has never allowed me to. It's like the scene in every action movie when the good guy gets knocked out. The screen goes black but then he wakes up somewhere completely different. Yeah, that's me but my brain is the bad guy that knocks me out and drags me somewhere I don't want to go.

Blood is sliding down the blade of the knife to the hilt, then dripping to the floor. I need to end this in a timelier manner. The puddle's diameter and depth are increasing faster than I'd like. I don't want to miss the moment he lets go but I feel the need to monitor the knife that protrudes from my side. Eddy stabbed me pretty deep and I'm wondering if any of my vital organs are punctured.

Some people are just so ungrateful.

He's been talking about dying for years and now he fights it. I will never understand people. If you don't want something, don't ask for it.

I'm still looking at the blade in my side when he stops moving.

Shit, he's gone, and I missed it.

I try C.P.R, still dead.

"Fuck!" I say, trying to stand up as the fabric of my shirt tugs on the blade. The pain is nauseating. Maybe tonight I'll die.

Time isn't linear but this is where we can start.

Blink.

"Everyone, I'm so glad to see you all on this rainy day. I hope your week has been full of victories and joy."

On Friday evenings, I go to a small support group for people who have suffered violent trauma.

It's a nameless gathering.

We all meet at Dr. Tobias' home. Home isn't exactly the best description. He lives alone in an abandoned hotel. Mold and dirt, everything has a hint of green and brown to it. Everything smells like mildew and rotting wood. The floors creek and the doors lean against the frames. Seven floors of empty rooms. Ten acres of ghost town on the very edge of the city.

"I am thankful to see you all have returned and not given up hope in each other and the progress we have made to this point."

Toby's grandfather purchased what had been a textile mill and, after dumping every penny he had into it, turned it into The Lux Hotel and Cottages.

The mill had closed years before the purchase due to a tragedy. Most of the time someone in that day would get their hair tangled in the looms and lose part of their scalp or die from Byssinosis. The body would be "removed" and no one would ever hear about it, but when thirty people die at one time because the opening room wasn't shut off from the rest of the mill and years of cotton dust and dirt buildup lead to a combustion as one spark from who-knows-where sends the whole place up in flames, it became a bit more difficult to keep things quiet.

"I think we should start with a moment of silence to center our thoughts and clear our minds of negativity."

At the time he purchased the mill, a river flowed directly behind it. The river powered a breastshot waterwheel which turned a line shaft that extended the full length of the ceiling of the mill. The line shaft would turn millwork that powered hundreds of looms.

The river that flowed from the city was eventually diverted to provide water for

countless apartments and businesses and soon
went dry before it could even reach the mill.

All beauty fades when exposed.

Everything wonderful dries up when people find
out they can use it.

Everyone wants to take a piece of the river
home with them. They want to put a piece of
the country on their mantle to stare at and
think of how wild it is, how untouched and
beautiful it is. Then suddenly the country and
the river don't exist anymore. They just flow in
a thousand sinks, sit on a million mantles, as
everyone stares and whispers.

"Look how wonderful," they say. "Look how wild
and majestic."

I couldn't care less about it, but I know a
trend when I see one.

Silence.

The doctor's grandfather. He poured every penny
of his fortune into the mill and the old mill
worker's village to turn them into The Lux.

He said that it was his dream to have movie stars and princesses frequent his suites and cottages. He wanted it to be something for his son and his son after him to inherit and make their own fortunes from. He wanted them to make a new name for the family, to start over in this new country.

That never happened.

"All right, we will start from my right. Quinn, how have you been since we last spoke?"

What he ended up leaving behind was alcohol addiction and a habit of torturing children.

The Lux became a prison for the family and a haven for addicts and prostitutes. The cottages made perfect little whorehouses complete with a shower and kitchenette, perfect for pimps because the merchandise never had to leave work or go out of sight. The city didn't care either because as long as the ten acres of heaven kept the city's trash it could easily be monitored.

Both grandfather and his son died young. The doctor inherited the prison and began to rid the grounds of unwanted guests. He just wouldn't give it up and eventually after ten years of stab wounds and begging, fighting and petitioning the police and local government to act, he had what some might call a victory.

And this is where we meet.

The Hotel he was tortured in.

The land he bled for.

The prison he won't let go of.

"I'm doing better, I think. I mean I still have urges, you know, it's hard for me to say no when I think I can make someone happy or make a connection, but I only gave in twice this week. I still get so lonely when I can't sleep. A million people around me and I feel alone. But I've been using the practices you've taught us, and it gets me through. I just keep remembering what you say to us. Don't judge progress by how you feel, judge it by what you can do today that you couldn't do yesterday, and I can see the difference in my thoughts, you know? And like, I do think I'm better off today than yesterday, so yeah." Quinn says smiling and twiddling her fingers around a piece of hemp twine.

Quinn is the type of woman you want to meet when you want something beautiful and easier than two drinks and a movie. When you want to fuck but not exchange names. She's what Marylin Monroe would have looked like if she had wanted to be Janice Joplin. She's mother Theresa pimped out on a corner. All of the compassion, none of the purity. A strung-out Norma Jean, but with none of the money and no one sticking around long enough to tell her she's beautiful.

"That's wonderful to hear, Quinn. I am so happy that you are finding strength in yourself. You deserve to live a happy life. Trust the practices and as I will always say, you are not alone."

Well, almost no one. The Doctor tells her she is beautiful, and she smiles. Every piece of self-esteem he gives her makes one more of Quinn's admirers want him dead.

Self-esteem is only good for one person while

the lack thereof is a gold mine for everyone else. But every mine has a limit to what it can offer, and once everyone has what they want, they leave in a hurry.

"Eddy, how has your week turned out?"

By the way, the sweet ever understanding doctor, the calm perfect soul that he is, the heavenly blue-eyed saint of a man, keeps a flask of whiskey in his Harris Tweed overcoat pocket, one in his brown leather satchel and one in his left hand. He always has three: his, his father's and his grandfather's. I guess bad habits compound with each passing generation if not checked.

"I've been staying in more," Eddy somewhat mumbles, then realizing the weakness of his voice, straightens his posture and speaks clearly, "I don't go to bars. I stay in and read or write poetry."

You've met Eddy. He was a soldier. I know basically nothing about the military. He was a special ops kind of soldier. The one they send to places where the life expectancy after being spotted is the time it takes the other guy to pull the trigger. Medals, a couple parades and one medical discharge. He scored in the 98th percentile on the P.T.S.D. test. This is Eddy, the wounded soldier.

"I still can't sleep, and I cry most nights. When I close my eyes, I see and hear a past I want to forget, so I keep my lights on now. I stay in and read or write poetry."

This is Eddy, the broken record.

Eddy, the sad puddle of tears.

He's the car wreck victim you smother before the ambulance makes it to the scene. You know he's too mangled to ever really live again so you smother what used to be a face to save him from the pain of finding out he would be better off dead when he wakes up.

"If you ever need anything you can call anyone of us. We are all here for each other. We are all here to serve one another, because through serving each other we serve ourselves. We are a family." The Doctor reaffirms his statement with a kind smile.

"I know, doc. It's just hard for me to reach out when I'm feeling like that. I just…"
Eddy whimpers and throws his own fist into his temple, he takes a deep breath and continues, "I just don't know how long I can do this."

I feel sick when he speaks but I also love him, and when he calls, I answer.

"We understand, but just know that you are not alone. We all deal with the ghosts of our pasts. Just remember to be present and never hesitate to reach out. You are here and in this moment. You are cherished by those around you."
Eddy and Tobi make eye contact and Tobi smiles sweetly. Just as Eddy looks away to cry, Tobi's mouth twitches and he takes a swig from lefty. "Well, that only leaves one more weekly report and then we continue with moving forward."

And that's us. The fucked up little group of trauma victims, lost in our pasts and pains, wanting to hear a story worse than our own. Wanting to be in the spotlight for two hours every Friday.

These are my best friends, my family.

If I said I live in the city because I love it,
I would be lying. It's the noise. The constant
sound keeps me distracted, and I'm the type of
person who needs to be distracted. If I think
too hard, I black out and, blink, I'm somewhere
else. The noise keeps me here, but the noise
outside along with the noise in my head keep me
awake.

The phone is ringing.

It's one in the morning.

I know it's Eddy, but I hope it's Quinn. I
could use a beer, but a good fuck would be even
better, an okay fuck would do just fine as well,
but it's a Tuesday and Quinn blows the local
hipsters on weekdays. You know, the twenty-
somethings who moved here to be models or
actors. The kind of baby-faced boys with that
twinkle in their eyes. The ones that think they
know something no one else knows, like they are
the ones getting over on you. No one told them
that this isn't the city to get famous in and
the twinkle seems to fade when the doctor hands
them a bottle of Azithromycin.

It's all part of the *journey*.

I think that's why Quinn goes for them. She knows they will leave, and it will be an opportunity for drama. She will cry and scream and act as if she gave two shits about them, but ask her to tell you their names.

I know it's Eddy and I could use a beer, so I answer.

Blink.

"I never wanted to be a hero and I didn't care when I became a murderer, I could justify it in the moment because I was fighting for my country, I was fighting for something that mattered, that really made a difference but these dreams don't give a fuck about my conscience…"

The Penn Bar, a forgotten basement where forgotten people go to drink. I find myself here on sleepless nights with Eddy. Every surface feels tacky from dried pools of spilled spirits that are coated with dust. The only moving air comes from moving bodies that shuffle past one another in the near darkness. I am Dante watching the panderers and seducers make their dismal rounds and Eddy is the soul that cried out.

Eddy was born to the darkness of shitholes like the Penn but beyond defeated eyes and tired hands I can see a strength still holding on. This teetering strength is the only reason I give a damn about his sad stories. The cigarette clouds hang sullenly above our heads. Everything about this place is more understandable with Eddy a part of it.

"…not because we were cold killers, they picked us because we cared for each other. We'd die for each other." His lips curl to a lethargic smile as he stares at his beer like every bursting carbonated bubble is letting loose a wicked scene. I want to care, but frankly, the sadness of reflecting on past trauma gives me a hard on for another person's pain. A hard on for anyone's pain but at the present moment a hard on for Eddy's pain and frankly I'd fuck anyone.

"If you could shut up, I'd probably be able to fuck you." I said the words before I could think them. My mind seems to play that way. He probably didn't even really hear me.

"What the hell did you say?"

Okay, he kind of heard me. "I'm just saying that when you show someone who has control over you, your weakness, you are basically asking them to fuck you. That's how they used you. Through your love for your friends and comrades. You wear who you are on your sleeve man. That's why you were an easy brain to wash."

Most people will just glide over something they don't want to hear simply because they don't want to hear it.

Eddy's head twitches and blue eyes blink from a glass of beer to me. "You heard from Quinn lately?"

I'm not stupid. He wants to know if I've fucked Quinn lately, yes, I have Eddy. "No, I haven't."

"I was thinking about calling her. What do you think?"

I think she wouldn't answer, Eddy. I think she wants to hear your stories even less than I do. "You should. She'd be happy to hear from you."

"I don't know, maybe I will. I haven't been at the meetings the past few weeks. Maybe she doesn't want to hear from me. Why don't you say hello to her for me, you know, just to feel it out? Has she asked about me at all?"

You really shouldn't. "You should call her."

We are all happy you haven't been around. "I've missed you. It's just not the same without you."

Why don't you go ahead and fucking blow those depressed brains out already? "I'll talk to her on Friday and feel things out."

No, not before, during or after we fuck has she asked about you. Not once. "She really doesn't talk to me much so I wouldn't know."

"Yeah, well I guess I should get going. Maybe

I'll come this week." He downs his tenth beer and swings his leather jacket from the back of his seat to his shoulder. In another life, before the blood and pain, the death and torture, I imagine Eddy as a real badass. That's probably why he joined. He had been told he was a badass so much he believed he was bullet proof, depression proof, P.T.S.D. proof.

Blink.

She screams so loud I feel like my ear drums are tearing into pieces, but the harder I thrust the louder she gets, and I just can't seem to stop.

She yells my name.

She whispers someone else's name.

I couldn't give two shits less whose name she says and somewhere in the middle of this sweat and flesh, this pleasure and disgust, I remember Eddy. Eddy and his sad blue eyes.

"Why did you stop? Did I do something wrong?" Quinn says, her tits still slightly moving up and down underneath me.

4:6

I got lost again.

Oh, Quinn. This apartment smells like a feeling. The feeling of knowing you're trash but you still look down on trash for being trash. Thirty-dollar candles in a mold ridden apartment. One-hundred-dollar perfume sprayed on unwashed sheets damp from weeks of sex and dead skin. A twenty-dollar bar of soap unused. That same bar of soap unmoved and unchanged and I've been coming here for months. Trash covered by more expensive trash to make it feel less like trash, trash, tra…

"Are you even listening to me?"

She's putting her clothes on. I must be thinking too much. She was under me and now she is putting on her clothes.

"I said, 'I don't know what's going on with you, but I feel like I'm not making you happy.'"

I never asked her to make me happy because I never expected her to. The soap catches my eyes again as she paces back and forth. I wonder how long she's actually had it. How many times the bar has watched her walk past? The soap hoping to be used or maybe dreading it.

"Do you still even want me?"

Want is the right word, I guess. I don't need. I don't love. I don't even care. I'm on the verge of not wanting. Just one more self-deprecating comment and my ability to want will be temporarily replaced with complete indifference.

"Anyway, I'm going to the country for a few days. You know, that place I've told you about. You should come."

She has told me. The hippie camp site where we could spend a week tripping in a cow pasture. You know cows have one stomach? I always thought it was four personally, but it turns out their stomach is set up with 4 distinct compartments: The Rumen, Reticulum, Omasum and Abomasum. None of the four compartments have stomach acid which makes the grass and clover they chew into cud an excellent substrate for mycelium, particularly of the psilocybin variety. The spores survive the digestion process and when the cow shits, it leaves behind little brown and white hippie magnets. And that is where Quinn is going, to rifle through cow shit and trip to convince herself that she isn't shit.

Blink.

Eddy's hand grips my shoulder to steady himself, "I'll see you around. I know it won't be long until we can't sleep again."

"Yeah, Eddy," I say, in my mind still naked with Quinn. "I'm sure it will be soon."

The moment he walks out the door, the Penn devolves again into a shithole full of trash, drinking trash, to feel less like trash. I light a match as I walk out and drop it at the door. Maybe the trash will burn, maybe tonight I'll sleep.

Blink.

"The Pharaohs said they were descendants of gods." Tobit says, throwing a wrench to the ground.

Toby. In a room with exposed pipes and steel mesh floor we talk about the collapsing society of which we are a part. A dog cage of a room where every time you move there's an opportunity to bleed on something sharp and rusted.

"The Pharisees claimed they alone could interpret the Holy Scriptures. King David's scribes claimed he was a man after God's own heart. And we all bought it."

The heat in the degrading family prison gave up again, so here we are in the basement, more drinking than working to fix a problem. More talking than acting.

"Our leaders created God so that they could become gods to us. They knew if they could convince us to die for God that we would die, and worse, kill for them. That's how they get men like Eddy to waste their minds and bodies on the battlefield. They tell them from childhood that Jephthah and Samson were men of God and they tell them that these men fought for their home that was given to them by God and through this they make them believe in things like patriotism, and peace through bloodshed. Eddy could be so useful, but I fear he is far too deep in society's pocket to value anything outside of it. Anyway..."

Three flasks.

His, his father's, his grandfather's.

Tonight, they are all out in the open. One in each of his hands and one empty on the floor. His grandfather's is made of tin and crushed to the point he has to tilt it to one side so the whiskey can flow freely from the one place still not crushed completely. There's no engraving just an old tin can full of bourbon.

"We as a society cling to what we are taught from birth and never take the initiative to question what we have been given. If we question these things, we are called traitors, we are called unholy and unworthy of the seeming luxury that comes with being a part of the lie."

His father's is silver, shiny but scratched from years of heavy use. The engraving spells out "Lucia" across the convex front and roses wrap around the sides and fill the back.

Lucia only drinks tequila.

"We are made to pick a side: white or black, Muslim or Christian, cop or criminal. We forget that we are all human."

His is steel wrapped in a thin piece of leather. No writing, no roses, no dents. He says that he'll never drink it dry because as long as he can shake it and hear scotch, he hasn't become an alcoholic.

"Do you remember being told as a child how we live in the greatest country on earth? Do you remember our parents and grandparents saying how things used to be so much better? The music, the food, the way children were raised, everything was more perfect somehow. The religion of our leaders is to keep us looking backward because if we never turn to face the front, they can manipulate our steps and cause us to turn in any direction they like."

I have a bottle of rum, the cheap kind made from processed sugar, not sugar cane. There's a half-naked bohemian girl on the side. She is smiling at you, wanting you to drink with her on a beach somewhere far from the city liquor store that smells like piss and body odor. She makes the drink feel authentic, but you know it's fake. You know you're fake, so why does it matter?

"The visible point of physical difference is made the magnet for all sorts of imaginary ascriptions. Gordon Allport said that. His point is made when you look at the trends of the media. Last month, we were supposed to hate one group for their faith, now we are supposed to hate another for their lack of it, and it's all based on how they look. Our heads are so easily turned because we have been taught to ignore contradiction. We have been schooled in an ideology that says faith cannot, and must not, be explained and to ask someone to explain it is folly and sacrilegious."

The heat still isn't fixed, and we are so drunk we probably won't make it to our own beds. Tin whiskey and Lucia tequila lay empty on the floor.

"God doesn't need to explain himself, therefore, our leaders need not explain themselves." He shakes the leather covered steel, pressing it to his ear to hear the droplets sliding from side to side.

"Fuck you, senior!" Tobias shouts as he jams his tightened fist against the low hanging ceiling. Blood dripping from his hand he smiles at me and says, "Still not a drunk."

We both laugh as I hand him the fake rum.

More drinking.

More talking than acting.

"Maybe we want to be lied to. Maybe it makes us less accountable for our bullshit decisions if we have someone to blame. Our leaders know this, they have always known it. We want to be lied to so that we don't have to take any responsibility." Tobi raises his head to the ceiling and shouts, "Hate to break it to the sheep, but when the rivers dry up and the plants stop growing you can blame whomever you like, but you and your shepherd will both be fucked!" He downs the last of my factory-processed rum and sits down with his head between his knees.

"Or maybe," I say, "It's just negligence. Maybe there IS no master plan. Maybe people just do what brings them pleasure."

After a few minutes of silence, Tobi says, "I can tell you all night long what is wrong with the world. But most of us have no solutions on how to fix it. That's the real problem, isn't it?"

Blink.

Every morning I woke up to Lina. She seemed to mourn the coming day. Stale cigars clung to the air from the open door.

I push forward through the haze, Lina still calling, mourning, echoing through the layers of stagnant air, air so thick you feel alone. That's why we never spoke. The air wouldn't allow it.

Mother looked like a Renaissance painting, always so beautiful. She was made up and shining, like a Humphrey Bogart dame, but actually an officer's wife. Really, she was just needing attention even when the cameras weren't rolling, even when the other wives couldn't see.

The air kept her silent as well. The boiling vapors from a meal simmering on the fire, the fingers of fragrance from wildflowers curled back on themselves in fear of being seen by the ash and smoke. All beauty kept silent, only the cigar spoke, the smoke and sting from the void beyond the open door.

Brothers.

6:1

Sisters.

Self.

All without sound. The shining black alone can speak.

Lina still sings from the void beyond the open door.

He fucking knew!

I want to hear a skull crack, feel warm blood on my feet, taste copper on my tongue.

I saw it in his eyes every time she complained about the pain, every time she cried in the morning. He would look at our mother, smoking a stemmed cigarette with beaded feathers on her wrists. He would grind his teeth and his red jaw would twitch and he'd ask why.

"Why, Violet?"

"Why, Violet?"

 "Violet, why?" he'd say. Our mother would flick her stem over the ashtray and say, "Oh Roger, she's a child, what could possibly be more normal than a bit of chaffing?"

Why? Why? Why?

"Why is she crying, Violet?"

Mother, with her curler hair and windmill arms would say, "Oh Roger, she's a child. Any number of things could have happened. Who knows why?"

Why? Why? Why?

Pick, pick, picking my fingernails and curling my toes in my shoes so hard I could feel them crack. I wanted him to say he knew! I wanted him to beat me dead for what I had done.

It was my fault.

The Bogart Beauty taught me how, but it was my fault.

I didn't want it to stop, and that's why it was my fault.

Lina still sings through the open door.

Blink.

I always wake up sweating. My neck, back and jaw tight from my nightly convulsions. I don't really mind, I expect it and for some reason that makes it okay, at least I know what's coming. I resigned myself to pain long ago and it can be used, I promise you, but I have yet to find the means to do so. So, I walk the light polluted city in search of stars and asking myself endless strings of questions I'll never be able to answer. Almost every night this is my routine, until I either black out or go back to sleep.

I always end up at The Lux no matter what path I take through the city. My eyes stuck to the ground watching shoes and hands that pass by. I'm hoping I won't notice walking into the street as a delivery truck turns me into a landmark for offering direction.

"Turn right at the corner," one man would say, "you know, remember? That guy with all the blood and the truck?"

"Oh yeah, I know the place," says another. "Took years for the stains to go away. Thanks."

Sounds like a legacy to me.

Anyway, I always end up at The Lux as if the city was a circle made only for me.

Shit, maybe I am on a ring in Dante's hell.

"Fuck!" I yell looking up to see The Lux gate staring back at me, seeming to say the same thing. I turn around and start back to my apartment. I've got to stop thinking while I walk.

I've tried to get groceries and ended up here nine times before I could find my way to the store. My feet guide me here and my mind won't let me stay long enough to control their movement.

I usually just end up eating dinner with Toby and sleeping in one of the rooms. It was something different every night. The bed was made, and the sheets were red silk. The rooms were so gaudy, but they made me feel like someone else. For a night I was anyone but me, and I liked it.

I grew up never knowing where I was going to

sleep. I mean, I didn't exactly sleep outside, but my mom was less than loving and left when I was ten. My father was a militant man and had no time for a child.

The first time I came down a set of stairs to see my luggage packed for me and a bus ticket sitting atop them, my father was listening to The Devil's Violinist. The radio was just loud enough to be heard, just soft enough to coil around your attentions. The fabric of his chair shielded him from my view, all except his gloved hand and the meerschaum pipe clouding the air above him. His hand disappeared for a moment and as another cloud formed in the room, he simply said, "My boy, I give you the breeze as your inheritance. Do with it what you will." He never even looked at me.

As an adult I can't blame my father. He was unequipped to raise a son with such a problem as mine. He often seemed afraid but not of me. I think now that he was afraid of my brain.

After that I stayed with many relatives, but it always ended the same. Waking up, brushing my teeth and seeing my luggage by the front door with a ticket. At fourteen, I was sitting on a bus bench, waiting to go to the next home. A neglected trash can was spilling fly swarmed cups and candy wrappers covered in trapped ants. The ants were still pincering violently at the sugar, completely unaware that they were already dead. I stared at them, tearing their limbs from their bodies, writhing in their pleasureful death at my feet. It was the first time I had ever realized how insane this game I was playing really was. I had been sad, angry and even happy before, but I had never considered my future self and what he would look like if I maintained my current course.

I thought about those who had failed me, but then considered the fact that maybe no one could help me. Maybe I was the cause of my own dismissal. These were difficult things for me to wrap my fourteen-year-old head around, but either way I couldn't play anymore. I left my ticket on the bench and walked away.

Blink.

I wake up in a cold sweat, sobbing and sitting upright. I squeeze my eyes shut and rub my forehead to clear my mind before trying to figure out where I am. With my eyes closed I feel around. "Okay," I say to myself, "I'm on a couch in The Lux. Everything is fine. It was just a dream."

I open my eyes and realize that I am somewhere I haven't been before in the hotel. A massive storage room with dozens of looms and several sets of antique furniture with room to spare. The looms are charred and broken. Cobwebs cover the knotted strings that twist over every surface. The walls are exposed red brick and the heart pine rafters stretch across the ceiling that's at least twenty feet high. The layers of dust that have collected keep the room so quiet all I can hear is the ringing in my ears. The room smells damp and the air is stale.

I stand, trying to find the door, and as I look around the room, my eyes go back to the couch I slept on. Dark stains cover the surface, every surface of every piece of furniture in the

room. I stumble back in shock and step on feet
behind me.

"Blood, it is all dried blood. Hum. Now where
are my shoes?"

I turn quickly to see Tobias standing with a
sullen look on his face. I must look surprised,
because he smiles and continues with his
explanation.

"I woke up before you and made some coffee."
He points towards the antique furniture and
machinery. "The looms are from the explosion.
My grandfather wanted to keep whatever he
could from when the mill was in use, and these
were all that was left. The room we are in was
ground zero, so to speak, the opening room.
Cotton was brought into this room and the bales
were cut open and the cotton was put into piles
over there." He motions with his head toward
two large wooden doors on the interior wall of
the room. "Well, you know why the explosion
happened in theory, but that's not exactly the
whole truth of the matter." He turns and walks
to the door leading to a hallway and says, "As

I said, I've made some coffee, we can talk in the kitchen. The air is stifled in this place and, frankly, I don't care to be here anyway."

The coffee is steaming as we enter the kitchen, and the smell carries me to a seat near a Japanese drip coffee pot. Toby selects two white ceramic mugs from an industrial-sized wooden cupboard above one of the many kitchen countertops. He pours a cup for himself and me, then sits down opposite me. We sit in silence for a while, then he clears his throat and begins to speak, "I consider you to be my friend. I don't befriend anyone. Eddy and Quinn are good people, but I feel a connection with you that is unlike the one I feel with them." Tobias pauses for a moment. He spins the coffee in his mug and stares into it. I can tell he is trying to decide whether to continue or not. I'm starting to feel like maybe I don't want him to. He takes a deep breath, then looks at me and starts again.

"The furniture you saw was a part of what you might consider a hobby of mine."

He puts his coffee down and looks into my eyes and continues, "Rather, let me start like this. The looms, as I have said, were a part of the explosion that killed twenty-eight mill workers and two foremen. The fire spread and burned what was, at the time, the factories on site village, killing many others. But what no one else knows is that the explosion wasn't caused by the buildup of cotton fibers and dust."

"The man who built this mill had previously owned a humble homestead. The land had been in his family for several generations. They were able to support themselves entirely and they made the money they needed for supplies and maintenance with the extra food they were able to cultivate and raise. It was a meager living, but they were unaware that money was something that people coveted, and they were happy with the abundance that the land provided."

He went silent for a moment, then continued, "He eventually had to sell the land because monoculture and mechanized farming had started taking hold. As a matter of fact, this was one of the first places in the United States where mechanized monoculture was practiced, and it was devastating to the homesteaders and family farms. They were unable to compete, and so entire communities were dismembered. He sold the farm, and with the money from the land he built this mill."

"He went into deep debt with the purchase, but he and his wife felt that the mill would pay off. Within a few years they had many accounts. The mill was paying their bills and they were able to pay their employees well. They wanted to treat their employees with respect and dignity so the housing they provided was affordable and the company store never took anything out of the checks paid. They left it up to the employees to pay their own debts as they could. This was in stark contrast with other mills of the time. The owner was happy, and his employees were happy. Everything was going as planned."

"But everything must come to an end and, just as his farm had fallen to mega-farming, his textile mill started falling to corporate giants. The city was expanding toward the mill

quickly and his employees started to crave a
more luxurious life than the one they had. So,
as they wanted more money the owner's customers
wanted to spend less, even to the point of
threatening to take their business elsewhere
because of the better prices. He tried to
convince his customers that the quality they
would receive from the larger companies would
be far inferior, but they didn't seem to mind.
Once again in his life, efficiency had trumped
quality, and he was hemorrhaging money."

"During this time his wife had also taken
ill and needed constant care. He hired two
experienced foremen so he could be at home with
her and their thirteen-year-old son, knowing
that his business was taken care of. What ended
up happening was much different. The foremen
started rumors that the mill owner was taking
lavish vacations with his wife and spending
the profits that could be going into their pay.
At first, the rumors didn't take, but as the
city lights flooded the sky, the fancy cars and
beautiful dresses of the ever encroaching rich
gleamed on the village, and the people wanted a

taste. They wanted to gleam in the light. They stopped caring whether the rumors were true, believing whatever they needed to believe so they could become surrounded by luxury. They stopped caring about the past, in which the owner had sacrificed even his own pay at times to pay them, and started falling head-over-heels for pure greed."

"It had been months since the owner had visited the mill and his wife had taken a turn for the better and wanted to get out of the house. It was springtime and a picnic sounded like a wonderful escape from the house. She wore her most beautiful dress, styled her hair to perfection and wore her grandmother's pearls. She made her husband wear his finest suit and they spent the morning preparing a basket for their much-deserved day out."

"That same day at the mill, a young boy of about five was playing while his mother worked. I'm not sure if you know anything about textile mills but they are overpoweringly loud. You could scream and someone standing ten feet away wouldn't even notice. And that's what happened, the boy got caught in one of the looms and no one heard him scream. By the time they found him he didn't even look like a child. He was just raw meat on the floor."

"The foremen took this as an opportunity to take things to another level. While the child still lay in a puddle of blood and skin on the floor, they preached about low pay and workers' rights. They were about to burn the place to the ground when they heard a sound coming up the dirt road. The owner and his wife had decided to stop by and see their employees. The owner was excited to be back and didn't even realize that he hadn't communicated with anyone at the mill except the two foremen for his entire absence. Seeing the husband and wife dressed so elegantly, every story that had been told to the mill workers came true in their minds. They dragged the wife from the car and took her and her husband to the looms."

"They shouted for justice for the dead child and beat the husband, breaking many of his bones, they then tied him to a chair and set it in front of the dead child. They brought in the wife, who had been screaming for her husband, and they said, 'Now we will be even.' They first put her hair into the looms, then her fingers, then her toes. The mother watched as the wife bled to death on the floor. When all was said and done the two foremen stood behind the crowd with pale faces."

"When she died, when the only sound was the sobbing of her husband, the reality of what had taken place struck every person in the mill and silence fell over them. They untied the owner and sent him on his way. They said that all was forgiven and that no one needed to know what happened.

"'Everything could go back to normal,' they said."

"The broken man drove home and told his son all that had happened. He then hugged his boy and said he was sorry. He pulled a gun from a drawer, placed it to his temple and pulled the trigger, all the while staring into his thirteen-year-old son's eyes. The boy cried until he couldn't breathe. He wanted to die with his father, so he put the gun to his own temple and pulled the trigger, but the gun misfired. His sadness turned to a deeply rooted rage. He walked to the village and in the waxing hours of the morning after barring every door shut, he first set the mill on fire, then burned the whole village and murdered every one of his father's employees. There were thirty in all. The ones that escaped the fire, he gunned down. The children who ran towards the river, burning and screaming, he also shot down and, when he had no more bullets, he used stones, his fists and sticks. The sun set on that day as the fire smoldered out and no one ever heard from the boy again."

We sit in silence.

Coffee suddenly isn't enough, so I reach into my pocket and pull out my cigarette holder. I pop it open with my thumb and pull out a joint. I hold it up and Tobias grabs a lighter from a drawer beside him. I light the joint and, as the smoke rises, I think on what he has just told me. Why did he tell me this? What was the point? I don't understand what this has to do with anything. I pass him the joint and he begins again as he inhales the sweet smoke.

"What would you have done if you had been that boy?" he says, looking into my eyes.

"I think he was justified. I wanted them to die and it didn't even happen to me." I say while reaching across the table and grabbing the joint.

"Exactly," Tobi whispers. "He was justified in his own mind and he acted. He didn't ask you, as I just did, if he had a right to kill those people. He knew in his mind what he was owed, and he took it. Even if you had said he wasn't justified, it wouldn't change the fact that it happened. Justice is in the eye of the beholder. Even the mother of the five-year-old felt justice when the owner's wife was dying in the pool of her dead son's blood. Though we would look in and say this was not justice but misplaced rage, no one could have convinced her otherwise and in that moment, it was justice to her because of the crowd yelling for her to commit murder. Why did they do so? Because they

were justified in their own minds, so they took
what they were owed."

His voice, still soft, says, "The difference
between that boy and the mill workers is this:
People are mostly too weak to make up their
own mind about their own actions and lives.
They wait on someone else to justify them and
tell them what is right and what is wrong.
It makes them feel better to be a part of a
bigger group that will reassure them they are
living in a sanctioned manner. Majority rules
and everyone is waiting for a ride on the band
wagon. If we just follow the majority, then
we have nothing to worry about, all of our
mistakes are absorbed by our peers because we
were just doing what the rest of our group said
was right. And as long as everyone lives in
this way, no one can be blamed for anything.
We have two major political parties in this
country, do you know why that is? It's so that
we feel like we have a choice. It's to make the
sheep feel better about following because they
can say they stand for something. It gives them
something to argue about amongst themselves.

They argue about which side is better, the left or the right, all the while both sides head straight to the slaughterhouse. Our wars, our religious groups, and our politicians, they all are telling us we are better if we kill for the home team, and millions of us have died believing this lie. The mill workers are a representation of the mass. The billboards imploring high school dropouts to join the military, the pastors telling us that other religions are trying to destroy our country, our educators teaching us that we are the greatest nation on earth, these are all a part of the mass, the expanding in-group mentality that is plaguing us."

"The boy represents the few of us who answer questions for ourselves and reject the idea that murder is only okay if the law and government say it is justifiable. The ones who reject the notion that individuality is based on the preference of the masses. The boy did what was just for him."

I can't speak. I feel like the air is stuck inside me. I come to when I feel the cherry of the burning herb scorch my fingers. I fling it to the table and breathe deep. This is truth. I know it is.

I still feel like something is missing.

"Here," the Doctor says, pulling a J from his cigarette case, "Light another joint and think about it for a moment. You know what I am saying is right. You've seen it." As he speaks, I put the tip of the joint into flame and watch the twisted end shine red from the heat. I spin the filled paper around to get an even burn and notice a black line inside the joint, but still too entranced by thought I barley even notice.

Again, he speaks, "That's why you fall from addiction to depression so readily. You know that there is something missing, something you weren't told that is keeping you from being what you should be."

I drag deep on the end of the joint and fill my lungs to capacity. "The furniture, the blood," I say, breathing out the heavy smoke, "I…I still don't understand…"

He looks at me with his smile and says, "I have told you what is wrong with the world, but I have offered no solution. And without a solution you will simply forget what I have told you and fall back into your normal cycles. This is how it is. People complain as I have many times to you, but they never act. Well, my friend, my comrade, my brother, I can finally give you a piece of hope to keep you on the right track. I can finally show you that I do far more than just complain, and so can you."

His smile is so beautiful, and his eyes dispel my lingering doubt. I crave what he offers to me. A chance to be free of inaction, to hold a compass that I know leads true north.

My sight begins fading from the edges. I can't speak and he knows. The Dr. always knows, so he takes the silence away.

"My grandfather was a man who often found himself quite like you, in a place he hadn't intended to go. He would wake up in these strange places and find that most of the time he had done something he had not planned on doing.

Sometimes it was simply that he would wake up next to a strange man or woman. Other times he would wake up with blood on his hands."

The sour smelling smoke and steam from our coffee mugs mix in the air between us. The joint is almost halfway down. I go to take another drag and my arm won't move. In a way it seems detached from me and I from it.

Fade to black.

End scene.

....

Shadows

Shadows and a voice break me from my eternity traveling through void after void.

"Everything is based on perspective. What is good for one is evil for another. What is sweet for one is bitter for another. What is pain for one is pleasure for another."

I fade in and out of consciousness, but he is always there. His voice is the one thing that keeps me rooted in reality. Black fades to blurred color, fades to black, but Toby's voice is always there.

"A man smiles as he lays on a wooden table. His hands and feet are bound to the corners. The wood splinters under his back from years of moistening and drying. The splintering wood and bound man are in a deep cell made of stone. The air is hot and dry. A fire burns near his feet, the only light in the little cell."

From black to glaring light to black and back again. My head wants to carry me away, but his voice keeps me here, now, in a moment I cannot escape. For the first time, I know what it means to be bound to the present. But my mind fights the present and my body is aching from days without rest. And from the void Tobit echoes.

"A voice enters the room. A voice attached to a cloaked and faceless figure."

"'I have made you wait. I have allowed your fear to consume you, and now I come to take it away.'"

"The voice moves closer to the smiling man. A shadow falls across the bound body and moves to the fire. The sound of steel and coal fill the room, the shadows of the fire dance higher on the walls as they brighten for a moment, then fade again to their former light."

I sweat profusely and jerk as my mind begs me to allow it to take me away, but his voice stills me and keeps me with him. Tobi's words are all-encompassing. I need his voice to break me of this disease.

"The cloaked figure hovers to a steel table

beside the bound prisoner. He moves his fingertips over the implements that rest on the surface. Serrated and smooth, blunt and bladed, gripping and grinding, every tool resides there, under his fingertips, waiting to be used once more by his hands. He makes his choice and drags the blade across the surface of the table. He slowly makes his way to the man. The man lies unshaken and still, smiling with his eyes wide open."

My eyes clear for a moment and my stomach turns. I try to jump to my feet to vomit, but the Doctor's hands force my body to lay down. The sting of acid fills my throat. I turn my head to the side as the burning liquid projects from my mouth. My eyes fail again, and back to the black I fade. My guide alone is present, and his voice keeps me safe.

"The dark figure knows that the smile will fade when the blade touches skin. They usually scream before he even enters the room and beg before he even picks his tool. He has seen a smile once before when a man thought only of his children, but soon the blade will be deep in this one's skin and the smile will fade as it always has before."

The room is spinning, but I am still alive in this reality. My stomach burns, and my head aches from a night of smoke and ash. My mind is still in pieces, but the shards are coming together. I am seeing things clearer and clearer as he speaks.

"The smiling man thinks not of his wife nor of his children, but of the master who saved their lives. He smiles as the blade comes ever closer as he thinks of his gracious master."

I want to be free from myself. To be free from an uncontrolled mind. Free of pain and torment.

"The blade falls deep into the smiling man's skin with ease. The cloaked shadow doesn't even have to pressure the blade. His hands pull the blade down from the bottom of the bound man's sternum to his pelvis. All the while, the man smiles. The wound fills with blood that quickly spills over his sides onto the warped and cracking table. He feels the warmth of his own blood and rejoices with laughter."

Fear is leaving my body. I realize now all pain is fear and that fear is weakness. My eyes start to focus. Color is becoming more vivid than I ever realized was possible.

"The cloaked torturer pulls back in confusion. He places the blade, now red and dripping, back on the rusted table. He lifts a pair of expanding clamps and returns to break the ribs of the smiling man. The sounds of cracking bone and wet meat echo off the stone walls. Still the bound man sings praises. The torturer hears for the first time that the praises are not for some god but are for him. His skilled hands begin to tremble, and he feels a streak of fear in his own heart."

"The smiling man slowly speaks, 'Please, blessed soul. Do not stop but be vigilant and continue your good work.' The bleeding man urges, 'Do not be afraid, you are giving me a blessing which has no equal in all the earth.'"

"The torturer lifts the mask from his face to breathe and looking down at the bleeding and broken man says, 'Why do you praise me? I am taking your life in the most horrid way. What is wrong with you? Are you mad?' "

" 'Continue your good work, and I will tell you why I smile, or else let me bleed to death and you shall never know,' the bleeding man cries."

Just as quickly as my clarity came to me, it departs, and I begin to slip back into the darkness. Tobit takes a burning stick and delicately places the flame to a ball of tar resting patiently on a black-and-silver dram stick. He breathes in to his lung's capacity and blows the smoke into my nostrils. My body becomes soft again and my mind enters the stone cell once more. Again, I become the bleeding and bound prisoner. Again, I am relived of all fear of pain.

"The unmasked torturer places his covering beside the instruments on the steel table. He takes a barbed rod and places it on the open ribs of the dying man. He reaches into his stomach cavity, as the man, with eyes wide open, continues to smile and praise him for his deeds. He takes the small intestines and wraps them around the rod. A tear falls from his cheek and into the pile of flesh that rests under his shadow."

"The smiling man looks into his eyes and says, 'Do not cry, my friend. I will tell you why I praise you for your deeds and perhaps you will understand.' The fire light dances in the little cell as he speaks. 'I was lost, and my family was starving. We hadn't eaten for many days and we had given up hope. I was ready to die. I was ready to kill my family so they would not have to suffer.' His body convulses and his eyes cloud for a moment. The color returns to his eyes and he continues to speak, all the while his organs wrap ever tighter around the barbed rod. 'My master saved us, he saved me from myself and he saved my family from starvation. I have lived since with the knowledge that I could never repay his kindness and the salvation he gave to me that day. I knew that I would live my life in service to him and at the end, I would have never been able to show the depth of my loyalty and love for him.' Again, his eyes roll back into his head and his body convulses violently."

I fade from the cell to reality, shaking and foaming at the mouth. Tobias holds me down with his hands on my chest, and I awake in the pool of blood once more.

"He regains himself yet again, and taking the torturer's arm in his hand, says quietly, and with perfect love, 'When my master was to be charged and sentenced to death, I stood and took the blame for his sin. I gave up the honor of my name and the honor that my son might inherit, but that was still not enough. Only you have given me the opportunity to truly show my love. Only you, servant of the most high, have given me the chance to live in full devotion and die in true service to my gracious master. Do not cry, for you will be blessed with many mansions by God for the good thing you have done.'"

"With this, the torturer can no longer bear his actions. He places his hand under the outstretched ribs, and with the smiling man's hand grasping his arm as if to hold to life itself, the torturer rips his heart from his chest and falls to the floor, sobbing in anguish."

"This is the power of knowing yourself. This is the power of knowing who you should become. Fear cannot take you. Pain cannot touch you. You are your own and you may walk this earth free of the rule of law and of the fear you have been given by your ancestors. I will leave you now to roam the darkness of your mind. Feel every emotion and cast all into the pit. Only retrieve that which serves you. Only hold to yourself that which gives you power and strength. There are those that say suffering is something to run from. Utilitarians, Anti-natalists, Humanists, and many others claim to know that suffering is objectively bad and farther from the truth."

His voice softens ever further, "No, suffering isn't something to run from, it is a beam of light into which you must run. You will fall along the way, but run to suffering because the mastery of it is all that diminishes its power. Falling into it is the only way to subject it to your will".

"So, first find peace in the darkness, find
courage in the storm. Find strength in yourself
and then, when you are truly at peace with
yourself, run to the light. For in light, as in
suffering, the things which are unknown become
known. The things unseen, beheld. Goodbye, my
friend."

Toby's voice is gone, my guide has left me to
wade through the thick of my emotions alone. I
slip from myself, lying on a couch in a room
of the Lux full of opium smoke and the smell
of vomit mixing with sweat, to the tortured
man, lying on the splintering wood, dead beside
the weeping torturer, to the darkness below my
dreams.

There is nothing here, only silence and a black
substance, ridged beneath my feet. The fear of
utter loneliness crawls onto my feet like ice.
It moves over every inch of me, then injects
itself into my mind. Fear turns to panic. I
am shaking uncontrollably and, in the midst
of my self-inflicted attack, I am penetrated

by a feeling. More than a feeling, it is an awareness of emptiness that I have never felt. It is an awareness of more than emptiness. I become actively engaged with the reality of my own mortality but not as before when I felt fear of death, this is something entirely different. This active engagement is my soul realizing its connection yet maintaining its awareness of its anonymity with the rest of creation. I, all at once, feel separate and united.

The floor falls away and I slip into the black substance, sinking deeper and deeper until I simply float. I am not impressed by fear or anxiety or panic any longer. I have reached a moment where I know them to be useless. The time passes and I float motionless for days, months, years. Time becomes irrelevant. I become unaware of my fingers and toes, then my arms and legs. I do not feel my hair brushing against my forehead, my murmuring tongue is silent. My heart is all that is left.

Thump, thump, thump.

It is not my heart that is beating. I feel the ripples wash over me with every beat. She is here in the dark. The pulses of soundwaves become more and more simultaneous with the sound itself, and I know she has found me. I stare into the emptiness as the need for fear returns and I am assured of the weakness of my newfound resolve to control my mind. Her blue eyes suddenly appear from the rippling substance. They captivate me completely and freeze me to my core. Her red lips touch mine and her tongue moistens both with a slow circle. Her hot breath is all the warmth I feel. My peace has broken and instead of free floating, I start to drown.

Thump, thump, thump.

I hold my breath, but it is no use. I know I can't find the surface in time. Her lips turn to a sharp smile, her eyes still shining in the dark. My chest burns, craving one more breath. My vision blurs. I open my mouth to let the substance into my lungs. The fear of death pricking at my skin.

9:12

Thump, thump, thump.

Her hands appear from the darkness and pull my lips closer to hers and she breathes the breath of life into my lungs. She wraps her legs around mine and I feel the warmth of her body. I feel her heart beating through her breasts, her rib cage expanding under her soft skin. She is my fear, and she saves me to keep me alive so that I may know her more. Her lips still pressed to mine, her tongue slides into my ear and whispers, "I will give you freedom for this moment, but know that I only give it to you so that you may know true fear when I take it back." She pulls away from me and once again I can breathe. The warmth of her breasts fade. Her arms and legs release me from their embrace. The tongue and lips smile and vanish. Her eyes blink and disappear.

Thump, thump, thump.

Her heart lingers in my ears, it pounds throughout the eternity around me. The ripples of sound pound at my chest, then silence. My body again departs from my spirit. I become a thought and nothing more, nothing less. Simply existing. Conscious of nothing but the moment. Lost but not needing to be found. A pure thought existing freely in a vacuum. Peace. Fear and anger depart once more and faintly I hear,

Thump, thump, thump.

I awake in the chamber, inside the dead, still bound to the splintering wood. The fire has almost burned out, yet the torturer still cries on the floor. I linger here for a moment, trying to feel the fearlessness of this man who knew his destiny and ran towards it. He is gone and now I only inhabit a corpse, so I keep moving to the light.

I blink and languidly wake in the Lux. The room is empty. Beams of light shine in from behind the closed curtains. I sit back on the couch and gain what is left of my mental strength in quiet contemplation. The moments pass and I realize I can no longer think, I am spent in every way. I just want to sleep. I just want to close my eyes and rest. I stand, gripping the armrest to steady myself. My stomach turns and I gag, but my stomach has nothing left to give up. My feet stagger to the door and I lean on the frame for a moment. "I'm still so weak," I think to myself, "but at least I had a moment of peace. That's a start."

As I leave The Lux, I look back at the building and notice from the corner of my eye that Tobias is watching me from the window of the fifth floor. I can't talk. I can barely move. So, I act as if I did not notice and walk away. Maybe I'll call Quinn.

"I would like to talk about dreams."

Dr. Tobi leans in and sips from the tin whiskey.

His hands shake slightly, and his eyelids are black.

None of us sleep.

We all have our reasons.

"Sigmund Freud believed that someone's subconscious thoughts and the motives for their actions could be determined by simply listening to them recount their dreams. He believed that our deepest fears and the reasons for our neurosis lay in the details of the visions we witness during our sleep."

Eddy doesn't sleep because of the war.

"We must look at our dreams as a way to gain insight into our own minds, nothing more. We can't help what we dream, and we should not judge ourselves for what we dream."

Quinn doesn't sleep because of countless beatings and the memories of every rape she's survived.

"We cannot become slaves to what we see in our heads and believe that we are somehow flawed or damaged because of our pasts."

I don't feel most of the time, so I can't sleep.

Allow your mind to become mine for a moment.

When you feel nothing, the basic needs of existence seem arbitrary and useless. Food loses taste, water doesn't quench your thirst and trying to rest is a waste of time.

You drink to feel and for a while you do, but over time the numbness creeps in again.

You take pills.

OxyContin, Xanax, Percocet.

You swallow anything that might get you high.

Valium, Suboxone, Morphine.

For a while you stay high. For a while, the sharp edges smooth out and you feel, but soon the sharp edges return and your tolerance for the high outweighs the flight and you crash.

You swing between addiction, tolerance and depression. You start to realize that the closer you get to exhaustion, starvation, death, the closer you are to feeling something real.

You don't eat for days.

You don't sleep for weeks.

You try to break yourself in new ways, hoping the pain will continue to overpower reality. You step in front of cars, you jump out of two-story windows for fun, hoping that you'll keep feeling alive. But even these extremes become boring with time and the cliff edge, the line between life and death, becomes tolerable.

Addiction, Tolerance, Depression. Repeat.

"We must not allow ourselves to become isolated and feel as if we are alone or broken or irredeemable because we cannot control our dreams and thoughts."

So, you give up, on feeling anything, you give up on life, but you don't really want to call it quits either. You're just floating between consciousness and a dream.

Then you turn a corner, walking to some trauma victim's anonymous meeting on a lonely street and a drunken bum knocks into you. You've had enough of their shit. They smell like shit. They look like shit. They live like shit.

Shit.

Shit.

Shit.

You try to beat the shit off him, but you realize that it is deeper than the surface. The filth has been a part of him so long, it's deeper than skin.

So, you dig in.

The deeper you dig, the more you start to feel. You feel, but at first, it is just release. Then, as the sounds of pian become louder, release evolves into justification. You know the pain is deserved. You know he needs it to understand a higher truth.

The truth that every decision he has made has led him to you. You are the judgment he has been sidestepping all these years. Suddenly, you are the light to cure the darkness. The warm blood on your face might as well be the sun. You are your own God.

You are his God.

You are no longer a tool to be used by someone else, some other god, you are your own tool to be used to devour what you deem unfit to live. The wasted piece of shit you are grinding to sausage is the chance you need to control life and death. The blood of the beggar is the sacrifice you need to feel again. Suddenly, you have found your purpose. But you were too eager to feel and as his chest becomes still, you realize you missed your moment to become a real God.

He is already gone, and you missed the moment.

You are alone again. Your heart pumping blood

like an engine pumps gasoline. Your breath is the exhaust in the cold air. You are a machine controlled by your own will.

The street is the same, but you are different.

You know who you need to become.

What will Toby think?

Blink.

"Lina Cavalieri 'In Quelle Trine Morbide'."

"What?" Eddy sits half naked next to me on his couch. We both stare at a print of Salvador Dali's Skull of Zurbaran. Our heads and hands are motionless, our eyes planted on the gloss print.

"The most beautiful woman on earth. She was an opera singer from the late eighteen hundreds on up to the thirties."

"Yeah, I think I know her. She did a few movies too, right?"

Our eyes locked on the figures seemingly praying to the skull. Their heads covered for fear of seeing the face of God, yet their bodies crowd ever closer to His form. The smoke of a smoldering blunt rises between us and the pandering souls.

"I hear that song in my dreams. It comes from a dark room. It's beautiful, but I'm too afraid to cross the threshold of the doorway," I say slower than I expected too.

As we speak, the reality of our surroundings

begin to creep into our hypnotic meditation.
I see the frame of the glossy print, white
plastic, warped and cracked. Then the peeling,
eggshell paint surrounding it filters into view.
The wooden wall behind the cracking eggshells
has water stains and is splintering, rebelling
against the form it had been nailed to hold.
Our eyes still stationed on the six robed
worshippers. The smoke still separating us from
them.

"You know what the doc said about dreams. Maybe
you should go into the room, ya know, see what
you're so afraid of."

I know what I am afraid of.

I am afraid of the god that lives in the dark.

I am afraid of becoming one of the worshipping
teeth in the painting, devouring myself as
an act of worship, being close to only what
God would have me rend rather than heal. I am
afraid of being a tool and not knowing it. The
monks pray for peace and yet they are teeth. We
huddle close to God for protection and become
the object of devastation we hid from.

My view widens and I see torn and dilapidated furniture, leaning to one side or sunken in the middle. I feel the subtle bounce of the couch under me.

"Shit, yes!" Eddy says, half whispering, half screaming.

From the corner of my eye, I see Eddy.

I see long blonde hair around his thighs.

I hear lips on skin. I smell perfume.

"It's just a dream. Maybe I'm just afraid of the unknown."

"Fuck, yes!" Eddy yells. The blonde hair whips to one side, revealing a smiling face. She looks at me, winks and leans back on one hand. The smell of lighter fluid and ash fills the room. I pass her the red-tipped roach. She breathes in deep, the cherry ever brighter against her smeared red lipstick. She opens her mouth wide and smoke filters through the light coming in the half open curtain and settles in the stagnant air.

"I think you need to smoke another joint and stop thinking about that shit." Eddy laughs while breaking up the sweet-smelling herb on a plastic rolling tray, his pants still below his knees.

The smiling lips laugh but never speak. I take the herb filled paper and fade again into the skull.

Blink.

"Remember," Tobit says, pouring the final drops of Lucia onto his tongue, "it's only a dream after all and whether or not those events have happened in the past, they are not happening now and there is victory in awaking. There is victory in being here today, in being in the present. I look forward to seeing you all next week. Have a wonderful evening."

As I listen to Toby speak, a smile crosses my face. Just hours before I was still lost in numbness and boredom, settling to waste my life fearing gods. I was ready to get lost in a painting, to lie to myself about being helpless and lost.

"I'm not afraid anymore," I whisper.

I know who I am now.

Blink.

"You beat him to death. And your next blackout wasn't for two days. He was a bum and, by the way you described him, I do know of him and I agree that you did him a favor, but the want to change is necessary when in the search for peace and unity with both passion and reason. We are driven by each and, as one man said, we must 'despise passion and master pain' to overcome the negative passions such as hate and pride, but I also believe we must use positive passions such as love, hope, and the like to overcome the indifference of lonely reason. Only through balancing these, may a person move themselves across the disparity that lies between the 'lost' and 'found' states of mind."

Tobias stops slowly pacing the kitchen only long enough to gain my eye contact, then looks away and continues speaking. Not to me entirely but I had the feeling I was supposed to be keeping up.

 "This isn't what I had in mind, but if we want to succeed, we must use what works." Tobi stops pacing and looks at me once more.

"This must be managed. You must listen to me.
If this is the path that heals you then we
will tread it together, but we must be a team,
otherwise you could become much worse than you
dreamed you could be."

"Listen," Tobi says quietly, sitting next to
me. "He wasn't worth the air he was breathing.
You did the city a favor, but these things must
be planned and clean. You won't just happen
upon people like him when you need to purge
your inner self. This was luck but I am here
to guide you." He drinks the last drops from
tin whiskey and places his other hand on my
shoulder, gripping it tightly. "How are you
feeling about what happened?"

I feel like a god.

"I'm not sure. I guess unburdened."

"Huh. Was there joy in it? Did you feel
powerful?"

The silence turns into a substance hovering
over the stainless-steel prep station. I can't
speak.

"Well," he whispers, "I will show you how to keep it clean, untraceable. But you must find a line and build a code for yourself. I can't tell you where the lines are, and I can't build your ethical framework, you must find them, and I would suggest quickly. And friend, don't find your line by crossing over it. You won't come back from that."

I will never forget the pain and sadness in his face. But I only cared for my own reasons and my emotions were unaffected by his trauma.

He has crawled to the doorway now and the sound of his grunting and sobbing, the trail of blood caused by the hole in his head and the twitching of his frightened body does touch me, but I remember his smile and his beautiful blue eyes as they were. The present is a memory, and I will always keep him there, smiling beautifully at me.

Everyone is me.

I can smell the bum from around the corner. I don't even need eyes to know what is coming. In a way it is comforting. The smell of sour clothes and sour breath, layers of the city's residue clinging to fabric and skin. I take it in with a deep breath, it almost burns as the smell goes down my throat, and I imagine all the particles that will linger in my lungs even after my senses stop detecting them. It is the future moving toward me, and I am time moving through the streets.

"Some pity on an old man?" The sound comes from shit-stained lips and the plea itself from eyes red with bursting blood vessels and yellow from a liver pushed to the brink.

Everyone is me.

I stare into his empty cup, "Ahh, I see," He says fighting his own breath. "You lost it already. Whatever pity that was in you now belongs to a million souls, young blood." The old man laughs, and his rotting teeth shine in the yellow streetlight.

"But what you don't understand, boy, is that you and I are the same." He motions with his eyes to the cup in his hand. "My cup empty too. I ain't never met no man with a full cup, but so much lost you almost empty? Ooo boy you better do sum bout that."

The smell is now a part of me, and my eyes, taking in the scene, keep my feet and mind in a kind of locked state.

He laughs again and halfway stands, pulling himself up on the greasy edge of a dumpster. His pants are already halfway down. He puts a bag under his ass, takes a shit in it and twists the top of the paper bag closed.

Everyone is me.

"You know, if it's too good to be true it probably is, boy. I see. Don't think I'm blind just cause I ain't here, ya feel me?"

He opens the bag and presses it to his mouth and inhales. A low rumble of an exhale releases the words, "You think you're so much different than me?"

He slips and falls to the pavement, as he laughs again, half-naked and half dead. I stare and wonder if he'll die tonight, "You think taking yo own shit is bad, young blood? I see what life is. I see how the others walk by like I'm the gutter. Like I'm the mutha fucka who don't know. Like I'm the one sufferin! I ain't too long now, so sit the fuck down so I can give you something to think about."

His coughing has gotten worse. He probably needs a hospital, but he is right, I do not care but my feet will not move.

Everyone is me.

He stares at the bag and then back into my eyes.

He suddenly speaks in a voice as clear as any sober, educated man. "I haven't always been here, ya know. I could go back too if I wanted. My family used to come and try to convince me to be that man again. You know, the type of man that loves his kids and works hard and cherishes his wife." His eyes drift off into space and I can almost feel his life leaving him, but I stay still and silent.

"I probably have more money in the bank than you ever will. Several of the tallest buildings in this city were designed by me."

I don't know if he is lying or high, but everyone has a lesson to teach. I think his is just to show me death.

The dying man looks down to the bag and speaks quietly as if only the bag were listening. "I loved that woman."

He looks to me again and continues, "People say money will change you but what they don't say is that it also changes those you love, and I never expected it to be her."

He places the bag to his crusted lips and his eyes glaze over again. The masochist returns as the man fades.

Everyone is me.

"Everything taken must be replaced. Ya hear?" he says coughing blood onto the pavement. "For every gain there is a loss. For every triumph, a failure. The moon is a streetlamp. The cars are mountains. Your clothes are fields and animals. Your home is the home of a thousand creatures all of um scurryin up and down."

He closes his eyes and starts humming with a deep rumble, "Down, down, down like that old song my momma used to sing ta me. You take but you don't understand that you gotta give back cause the balance needs be, my son. The lights are on in one house while birds drop from the sky, while creatures you ain't even notice lose their way and die so you can read a goddamn book, boy listen! You got that empty cup cause somebody done took all you got but remember this," he grasps my shirt and pulls me so close I can feel the heat of his breath on my face, "because you empty, don't take. You ain't ready yet young blood, ugh!"

Blood spews from his mouth into mine and the taste and heat shake me. A tepid breath goes in and out of my body in sync with his. His eyes go wide, and a smile crosses his twisted face.

Everyone is me.

He is not dead, but why would I allow him to wake? Is this the turning point for him? No, this is below the bottom and I am a merciful god so with my hands around his neck I watch his chest expand and contract slower and slower until nothing exists, except the shit covered body of a half-naked man.

This is truth.

This is real.

He didn't need saving. He needed release.

Everyone is me.

Blink.

I wake up to the sun peering over the skyscraper outside Quinn's window. I wipe my swollen eyes and roll over to a still-sleeping Norma Jean. Her hair is covering her face and I know it is only going to take the sun another few minutes to wake her up, so I move purposefully. I would rather not wake her, but I doubt that is going to happen after last night. She will probably be sore for a week and I cannot remember the last time I enjoyed sex that much. My legs are like jelly. The sex was empowering and erotic and I could come back every night for a year and not get bored, but it did not touch the high I felt slaughtering that tortured soul. I need to find another. I need to set someone else free from fear.

I walk to the bathroom to piss and see a neat little pile of used condoms beside the toilet. My eyes circle the room. There is the same bar of soap still slumbering on its shelf, waiting to be used. I turn on the sink to wash my hands and decide to use the bar for the first time. Layers of scum have formed around the surface and I'm not sure if I am getting to the soap underneath. I try not to think about it too much and grab my clothes from the floor. Every board in the room creaks, so I make my way to the door and finish dressing in the hall.

I have never paid attention very much but now that I think about it I can't remember ever seeing anyone else in Quinn's building. It is like she lives here alone. No noise from the other apartments. No other smells. Just empty hallways and stairwells.

I am sure I have seen someone else, probably just didn't notice.

I get lost in my head a lot.

I can never smell her apartment until I leave. My clothes carry the scent into the outside world, and I become a mobile advertisement for patchouli oil. A walking hippie commune meandering through the city streets. I can't go home. I can't eat. I need to start my search now. I need to find my next sacrifice.

Part of worship is begging, but you won't hear anyone say that.

I am stepping in and out of the spotlights dotting the night street. The whole city seems like a stage to me. The vendors on their corner stage trying to sell their food. The men and women in suits with briefcases and valises trying to sell their illusions of affluence to the poor. The prostitutes trying to sell their bodies. Everyone wants a place on the stage so they can be seen and loved and bought. They want to be in the spotlight even if it's only for a moment, just as they walk underneath. The streetlights become spotlights and everyone gets their chance to be sold every ten feet.

I am looking for another soul to help me feel. The next high that will not let me down. I am looking for the first experience all over again but trying not to make it happen. I want it to fall into my lap, I do not want to expect it. I have gone in search of all the others and now I know the high I felt before was from the suddenness, how the moment had been thrust upon me. The first time was beautiful because my mind

15:1

was lost in despair and peace had found me, saved me.

I have been doing the city a favor by lowering the homelessness rate, but the boredom is finding its way back into my life. I need something different, something more satisfying. I crave a more perfect sacrifice.

I can't even tell you where I am. My feet keep a rhythm with my heart and my body follows both wherever they lead.

"You look like you're lost."

A silken voice calls my ears to attention. My eyes follow the pavement to red high heels. Smooth black skin shining on long slender calves move out of the darkness and into a city spotlight. Her thighs widen gracefully to hourglass hips, seductively held by a red cotton dress. I cannot move my gaze past her perfect figure. Lust and passion, my fingertips tingle.

I have watched her for so long and never saw that she was the one. The moment I needed to fall into my lap. I have only heard her speak once, have only seen half of her form and I know she is for me. I can smell her blood pumping through her veins. I can feel the air leaving her body as she breathes. I am underwater after an explosion and the shockwave hits me with the effect of a mushroom high, pushing me deeper into the water and further from reality. The smell of wet smoke and the sharpness of liquor guide me to her face.

"You looking for somethin, baby? I can help you find it if you come a little closer." She takes my hand. Red fingernails lead my eyes further across her skin, twinkling like the night sky on the city's perpetual stage. Red lips turn to a smile. Her sparkling blue eyes sizing up my intentions.

"Just follow me, baby. I'll show you where to find what you're looking for." She whispers the words, and they pour into my ears like water on a dry tongue.

I am the butcher being led by the cattle. I let her hand pull me into the darkness.

Far away from the sidewalk stage we walk alone. She talks along the way, but I am too busy thinking of how I want to make her worship me to hear a word. Too busy figuring out the details to care. My heart is pumping so hard it hurts to breathe. My legs are wobbling but I keep moving forward.

Suddenly we stop and I realize we are about to enter the ten acres of heaven surrounding The Lux. How had I not realized I was so close? I was sure I had been walking for hours. I knew I had to be on another side of the city entirely. It doesn't matter. I need to focus. I cannot let this moment pass without feeling every second.

We walk to a small cottage on the back edge of the property. I see a light in The Lux shining through an open window. Maybe Tobi is looking down on us.

As we approach the small building, I think of how peaceful it must have been with the river flowing behind it.

Blink.

The sun is shining on my face. The sound of whitewater opens my senses. My nose breathes in the fragrance of the white and untouchable magnolia petals. Two small boys chase each other around the massive trunk of a magnolia tree. A little girl with wind-blown hair in her face picks poppy pedals in a field of wildflowers. She places them in her palm and blows them into the breeze. She smiles and spins with her arms outstretched until she falls in the grass. The beauty in red sits on a swing under a stretching limb and the opening blooms of the tree. Her feet kick in and out moving her gracefully over the grassy hill and river's edge. I sit on a blanket watching the children laugh and dance in the warm spring air. Everything echoing with joy and peace. The blue eyes gaze and the red lips smile and say, "Here we are, baby."

Blink.

"Here we are. Come on in and we can find whatever it is you want."

The air is cold, the river is a dry gully filled

with trash and the tree is a trunk with broken glass littering the dirt around it.

I need to focus. This is what is real.

This is what I must become. This is how I feel again.

We enter the room and I close the door behind us. The cottage smells of mold and bleach. The door handle is slick from hands covered in lubricant, grasping it to escape their guilt. The carpet has small foot paths from the door to the bed, from the bed to the bathroom, from the bathroom to the door. Every piece of furniture has stains and hair lining the edges. The wall behind the back board of the bed is cracked and the bed frame has nearly given in to excessive use.

I take a moment to steady my mind.

Breathe in.

Hold.

Breathe out.

I turn from the locked door to make my sacrifice

beg before spilling its blood, but the lamb smiles as I approach and says, "I know what you're looking for."

The lamb limpidly states, "I see it in your eyes. I've seen it in a thousand eyes before, but it's buried so deep I know it could never reach the surface. But you, I see it in the black parts and the edges. It's in and around you. You're going to try to kill me."

I stop my advance as the red dress steps forward. The thin fabric holds tight to her form but is stretched from hundreds of hands tugging to see what's barely hidden underneath. Instead of her as the victim I now see hundreds of souls clinging to the fabric, trying to pull themselves from the pit as she calmly walks by.

"Then why did you bring me here alone?" I ask, once again moving forward and pushing a strap of the dress from her shoulder. I am sure that my advance will bring some of her fear to the surface but again she steps closer. She lifts her right hand and traces my chest with her fingertips. Chills run down my spine.

"I've seen it before," she says, licking her lips, "and I've wanted it. But they are all too afraid of the consequences. I see it on their faces, in their shaking hands."

She takes my hand, holds it up for a moment, then looks up through her eyelashes and smiles. Her blue eyes, her red lips, her wet tongue, that is all I see. None of them begging, none of them afraid.

"They're thinking 'what if' over and over and over. By the time they've gone through every scenario, the condom's in the trash and I'm out the door. It's a way for them to get off, you see. They can separate the sex from emotional attachment if somewhere deep down they want to kill me."

If someone is not begging, it is not worship.

If they are not on their knees, you do not own them.

If they are not afraid, then you are not really God.

"It's like meditation," she says, pulling on

the other strap to free both shoulders. "Like if they focus on killing me, they won't see their wives and kids while we fuck. But it's not about guilt for you, is it? It's about something else entirely."

She puts both hands through the straps and sensually lifts her arms above her head. The worn straps fall to her sides. She rests her forearms on a mess of black hair held up by a red ribbon. She pulls the ribbon as she lifts her arms straight, fingertips searching for the ceiling. The ribbon falls to the floor between us and the curls of her hair bounce to her shoulders.

"All you have to do is pull down on the straps and I'll be completely exposed, helpless. Is that what you want? Do you want me to beg you?" her lips pucker as she speaks.

She bites her bottom lip and moans the words, "Give me your dick, baby."

I feel my nose flare, my jaw tighten. She is toying with me. Why isn't she afraid? She knows what I want. Why isn't she screaming? Why isn't she clawing through me to get to the door?

"No, that's not what you want. You want me to beg, but not for you. Give me my life, baby."

My face turns red and my knuckles feel like they might break, my fists are so tight. I am flushed and feel embarrassment. How can she be so bitchy, knowing I control her life? I grab her throat and squeeze, gritting my teeth.

"That's it. You want me to beg for my life. You want me to cry? You want me to get on my knees," she says with a smile as she kneels at my feet, my hand still grasping her neck, "you want me to beg, beg, beg."

"Let me suck on your God complex, baby." She laughs and twists out of my hand before I can reassert my grip. She stands up ass first, arching her back and pivoting on one foot towards the bed. She bends over, left hand squeezing the comforter, her right pulling her dress above her waist. She whips her head around tossing her hair to one side and stares into my eyes.

All I see is blue.

I am starting to feel like I am the prey, not
the predator. I am the tooth, she is the mouth
I am stuck in. I am the tool again. I have lost
control and I don't know how to get it back.
Gods do not need to beg for control.

Gods do not beg.

"I'll do whatever you want if you let me live,
baby. You can have anything you want. Just
please don't hurt me. Please. Please. Please."

I am at the point of rage, but my body will
not move. I cannot wrap my mind around what is
happening. This is not what was supposed to
happen.

A god's name alone insights fear.

"Oh, baby," she giggles, "you had this planned
out, but only I'm not weak and afraid. In your
head you knew I'd be what you wanted, but guess
what? What we want is seldom what we need."

She turns around and sits on the edge of the
bed. She puts her hand between her legs and

unlatches a black strap. A spotlight shines through the open window and she is the star. The stage is black save the blue eyes, the red dress and her soft dark skin. Light reflects onto my chest from steel.

She stands and steps so close to me I can feel her heartbeat. Blue eyes and red lips, that is all I see. Feel. Hear.

Thump, thump, thump.

"Things don't always go as planned," she whispers. "I've been saving this for you. I just hadn't met you yet. But the moment I saw you I knew you were the one just like you knew I was the one. I knew you'd wake up for me, it just took some time, baby."

The blade pressed against her neck is tugging at her skin like the hands from her past lurking deep in her blue eyes, still tugging at her dress. The souls like mine begging for mercy as she walks past. I am stuck in my body watching her press the knife to her own throat.

Powerless. I want to beg her to stop.

Gods do not beg.

Thump, thump, thump.

"I want you to remember this. I was walking to my death when I lead you, boy. I decided to give you this moment. It's what you wanted, isn't it? To see me die. Well, I'm giving this to you, but it comes with a price, and here it is." She stands on her toes. The back of the blade presses against my jugular vein.

She whispers and with each word I feel her lips on my ear, "The price is knowing that you aren't God. The price is knowing for the rest of your life that you had no control over me. You have no control over anyone, ever." She leans back and her eyes lock again with mine.

"Give me your fear, baby."

She smiles like she knows the future. She smiles, not because she is happy, but because she knows something I do not. Her smile says, "I told you the end. I told you what you didn't want to know. I told you the secret you've been searching for."

I am not God.

The blade glides like a shark fin through water.
Smooth and haunting, awful and deadly.

Thump, thump, thump.

She grabs the back of my neck and pulls my lips
to hers. I feel her blood soaking my shirt.
We stand there for a moment, lips locked. Her
tongue feeling the inside of my mouth. My whole
body ridged with confusion.

Thump, thump, thump.

She pulls away and we stare into each other's
eyes. She slowly falls to the floor. I find
myself holding her in my arms, falling with her
into some abyss. Falling into the pit with the
souls she never saved.

Thump, thump...

With the spotlight still clinging to her form,
the blue eyes fade to gray. The curtain draws
closed and, suddenly I am alone. She is gone
and I hold her until stillness and silence are
all that remain.

15:14

The sun is rising through the window. The rays of light dance on her hair and face. I have been here beside her for hours staring at the red dress, the red lips. Unable to move past the moment she took my ability to feel. I stare with my mouth open, kneeling in a pool of clotting blood, trying to regain a piece of the self-assurance I had just hours ago. I am trying to convince myself that it was just a dream, that I am still a god, but her lifeless body holds power over me, and I can't move from beside her. Her words scramble through my brain like buckshot.

"Give me your fear, baby." she said.

I know what I am afraid of.

Addiction, Tolerance, Depression. Repeat.

You do not eat for days. You do not sleep for weeks.

When you can't feel, everything necessary to sustain life becomes arbitrary and meaningless.

She broke me and now I have sunk back to the depths of boredom and self-pity.

She took away my power. No matter what I do now I will always know that she took my control away.

God does not allow anyone to remain fearless in His presence.

Blink.

"What is the meaning of life?" Tobias questions the group after sipping from his leather-bound flask.

I hear bits and pieces of the meeting. Lately I do not even remember how I have gotten here. I wake up in the rotting mill wondering how long it has been this time.

Have I been out for days, weeks?

Sometimes I wake up smelling like Quinn, other times I smell like booze, even other moments I smell like weed.

My disillusionment only lasted for two weeks and now I realize that no matter how faraway I get from what I have been given, I am still just a rat in a maze, a tooth in a mouth, a slave to a better god.

"Some say it's to serve God and to be a messenger of his will to the world."

Most of you have probably judged me as insane by now. I can't argue with that. But I will say that seeing all of you sitting in your lazy chairs in your two thousand square foot houses, flipping through these pages waiting for a point to come to the surface, waiting for a twist to reveal itself, waiting to get some excitement because your life is just as dull and void of feeling as mine is, I start to think maybe I am the sane one. While all of you have been reading, I have been acting. While you have been trying to figure me out, I have been trying to find myself at any cost. Your fear keeps you in the same cycle your parents and grandparents perpetuated because their parents and grandparents perpetuated the same cycle their parents and grandparents perpetuated all the way back to the Fertile Crescent.

"Some say it's to try to live peaceably with one another and gain wisdom from our experience and the experiences of others."

I can't judge you, I guess. At least you have a direction you are following. I just wade through the noise, not really hearing anything. It has all become a blur. I had found what I knew was right and she took it from me.

"Others still, say that it is to seek knowledge and build something from that knowledge to leave to the next generation and so on."

I knew who I was supposed to be, and she snatched my meaning from my hands and threw it away with her life. I know how the Crusaders felt, the ones that took the six-month journey to the Holy Land in 1304 only to find out that the crusade they were seeking had ended. No one would ever write their names in any histories, no one would ever remember them. They had left their homes knowing who they were. They had known how they wanted to die, and some had even imagined the songs and poems that might be written about them. Yet they reached their fate to find it did not exist and they had been wrong. Everything they believed in had been a lie, and they had to walk back to the ship and return home a vanquished soldier who had not even fought.

"I've heard even others say that we are meant to conquer. Whether it be the world or other peoples of the world, we must conquer and keep climbing towards ultimate power."

I expected a warrior's welcome but now I am the Viking who never died in battle. I am the blind man who waited to be healed, but Jesus simply said, "You were meant to be blind, now leave me." I am weak and defeated.

God drowned the earth when he felt this way.

I wonder if she has been found yet.

"All of these beliefs have something in common. The fact that they all deal exclusively with human and divine interaction. What if they are all wrong? What if we are simply meant to live and die and tend to the needs of other creatures of the earth? What if we are not the prime rulers because of our intelligence, but the most suitable caretakers? If we come to this understanding, suddenly there are no enemies, suddenly we are free to enact a story of peace because we have no need to compete with one another. In this state of consciousness, we become insignificant in a way that makes us completely free to simply live."

I wonder if Trotsky felt this sad when Lenin called him a Menshevik and gave his job to a fucking sadist gangster. But he didn't seem to want power, maybe that's why he died in Mexico and not Russia. Lenin wanted power and blood, he got what he wanted. Am I just too weak? How many books can I read before I run out of head space? Not many I would wager.

"We must seek to become insignificant creatures of the earth. Flakes of skin fall off our bodies with every move we make yet we are completely unconscious of it. We are less than that to the universe that surrounds us. If we were to destroy the planet completely then maybe we would reach the magnitude of a single flake of skin falling from a human body in the eyes of the universe. We must lose all sense of divine purpose to be happy. If we see ourselves as this, then we are truly free. Society tells us that we are significant, and we have meaning and that meaning gives us our individuality and purpose, so we equate insignificance with uselessness and, in a word, unworthiness. What we should understand is that to view insignificance as such is to be lost in pride and self-absorption."

"My point to all of you is this: If you can shift your mentality to something like what I just stated, you may be able to free yourselves from the trauma of your past. If you free yourselves from divine value then you can free yourselves from guilt, shame and fear. And in freeing yourselves from these things you will be able to simply live without the pressure of needing to overcome and accomplish. Rather, you can simply exist in the understanding that what has happened is over and what is to come is unknown. You will soon be able to live moment-by-moment and day-by-day."

Aleksandr Solzhenitsyn probably thought things would have been different. It is those that go willingly, that do not put up a fight or make a fuss, that allow a society to fall into ruin, or something like that, but you get the point. I just watched in silence, in darkness and as naive as an innocent baker being dragged to a gulag.

"And don't rush yourselves to conclusions and become angry with yourselves for your lack of immediate understanding. St. Catherine Benincasa said that there is no sin nor wrong that gives a man such a foretaste of hell in this life as anger and impatience. So be calm and simply take one step at a time in your journey. Simply live and better the world that is around you and I promise you will find peace."

I am not God.

Blink.

"The police have been frenzied on the east side of town, you know."

Tobias is sip, sip, sipping and staring out a window, looking down upon the cottages rotting in the rain. "You know as well as I do that small thinking leads to small action," he says in a disgusted tone, as if he should not have had to say the words at all.

"It is a small matter," he says turning towards me with a smile. He puts out his hand that holds Lucy and gestures with his eyes for me to have a drink. I take the flask as he clears his throat.

"You see it, don't you? The others are degrading by the day and I see that our project has started to interfere with their progress. I'm not an evil man, though, am I?"

I know I am speaking, but the lips that move are disconnected from my mind and all it shows me is blood sticking to everything. Lucia is covered in it, and when I hand it back to Tobi it sticks to my palm. Strings of red connect my hand to the flask as if it were clinging to me.

17:1

Tobi's teeth are covered in blood, and even his beautiful smile cannot bring me from the dead place I have been made to inhabit.

Time is condensing. The sun will rise soon.

Have you ever stared at your own hands? If you stare too long, they start to look foreign and disconnected. You feel in that moment that maybe you don't understand the world around you as well as you previously thought. Maybe that's just me.

"Yes!" Tobias slams his hand against the wall with enthusiasm.

"Yes! You have been listening to me. I so often nearly lose hope and you always seem to pick me up, old friend. But we can't waste time on these subjects now." His smile quickly fades and his demeanor changes from that of a close friend to one of a firm leader.

"You are experiencing your journey on your own terms and I will not interfere. I will only say this." His hand falls on my shoulder and I am brought to the surface again, like ascending from the bottom of an ocean and, upon arriving to the surface, I am clean, filtered. He pauses for a moment as if seeing something he had not before, but continues, "Remember the Why."

His hand lifts from my shoulder and glides through his hair to push it from his face.

"There is more work to be done. And you have much more to learn. Buddha was right when he said attachment is pain, but I don't believe he ever truly rid himself of it. To do so you must relinquish that which you love most. And then, what you love most after that, and so on until there is nothing left but all you hate. Then you must destroy those things as well until there is nothing left. Then destroy the things that mean nothing to you because once all else is gone, once all you love and hate have been eradicated, you will begin to attach to something else, anything else. It is human nature and everything you see must be destroyed until there is nothing left!"

Tobias grabs my hand and pulls me near, our foreheads touching, and our eyes fixed, his other hand grabs at my hair to press us even closer and asks, "When do we stop?"

Then together we say the words that would lead me here.

"Until there is nothing left."

There will be things I do not tell you and questions that will go unanswered but what I am trying to accomplish is to distill years of my life onto these pages. I am trying to give you the pieces that matter most to me.

I have nothing left and no one will remember my name, not even you, dear friend. I am a lost person in a sense because I could not see through my own eyes for a long time and the part of me that took over was disconnected from the ground and therefore floated from here to there with no roots to plant him. I am the cause and inspiration of some of the most terrible crimes. I am also a victim. Yes, I committed many unforgivable acts, but those who were spurred on and committed acts of their own were not followers of mine. They used my carelessness and obviously diminished state of

17:4

mind to allow themselves the liberty of acting as they wanted. At any time, I could have been stopped but I was not and also… I did not.

Blink.

How long is this sustainable?

I picture myself as an old man with nothing but
quotations to say, and a handful of them for
any situation.

How long is this sustainable?

I never really know where I am. I never really
see my own body. I cannot remember the last
time I looked in a mirror.

How long is this sustainable?

I only ask because no matter how much you know,
you can never make anything permanent, which
means in one sense you will never know enough
and in another, nothing is sustainable.

Is God sustainable?

God created everything and is apparently
eternal, so what does that mean? How far apart
are the thing which is sustained and the thing
which is eternal? How can a clear line be
drawn? Does something go from being sustained
to being eternal at a billion years? Certainly
not because we already know the earth is older

than that but is not eternal. So, is it ten billion years? One hundred billion? One hundred trillion? You can only know something is eternal once eternity has passed but then, what is eternity once it ends?

How long is this sustainable?

Eternity is not confined to the future but also belongs to the past. Its very nature excludes time from the paradigm completely and renders our conception of it meaningless. Your watch, your phone, your fucking alarm. You listen to them and accept them because they match your view of reality. When someone says the year, you do not even flinch because you need to be anchored, you need to know your place, your time.

How long is this sustainable?

So, is it not true that all things are sustainable, but nothing is eternal? Eternity is pliable in our imagination for the fleeting amounts of time most people spend thinking about the word. Pliable enough to make peace with. But I have thought about this word every day for years trying to make sense of it. Not for its own sake but to feel a grounding in a word so common yet so incomprehensible. I try to find comfort in the date, the time. If I know when something began then I can place myself in the center of it.

How long is this sustainable?

I have thought about love, a word so abstract that even saying it recalls something almost ethereal, something intangible yet something everyone claims as their own, something fragile and also enduring. I have spent my nights for months and months looking into mirrors and acting out facial expressions, hoping there is a feeling I can find in them that makes them spontaneous to others, stretching at the corners of my mouth to find happiness. Words are sounds that plague me and their meanings supplement my brain with just enough understanding to find my place among you. But none of you mean what you say. You only speak what culture whispers into your ears, and you accept it so that you can move on. The axioms are enough for you, but I cannot stand on them.

How long is this sustainable?

But really, I don't care, and my point is not about time. My point is based on logic and how we arrive at conclusions. In other words, what are you willing to believe, and secondly, how much proof do you need to believe it? If you say, "Well, what is proof?" then I have no time for you in this story and you will have to decide that on your own. I want you to know that if you keep this in mind my actions will make sense. If you do not feel empathy towards me, I understand. My life is fragmented and redundant. I must believe I have a reason for my actions and that, for me, they make sense. What reasons do you have? What data set are you working with that leads you to conclusions? If you think about these questions for any length of time you would also see the flaws and biases in your convictions about what surrounds you.

Fuck, I can't keep ranting like this.

Blink.

There is a feeling I get, like a hook going down from the top of my skull into my brain, through my amygdala and down my spine. The feeling that something is stuck inside of me and if I try to pull it out the barbs on the hook take everything out with them. I start pulling on the metal and the upper barb touches the top of my mouth.

"If I just pull harder it will be over with." I tell myself, but I know that without the hook, I will not be tethered to this place anymore. My hands are covered in blood and grey matter from the last time I attempted to dislodge it. My chest still aches. I've felt it my whole life, known it was there but no one has ever had an explanation. Some say I am lying for attention, others say my diet, others say, others say, others say.

The eye of the hook sits on my skull and watches the world around me like a third eye. Its purpose is to see danger, to find it and alert me to it. When it sees this danger, it shakes violently and sends a vibration down through the throat of the hook around the bend and into the barb that scratches my sternum with a claw-like tendency for causing pain. I have tried to have it removed. I have tried to pull it out, but my hands are still covered in blood and my body remains sore from every attempt. My brain tells me that the hook is my friend. They have been a part of each other for so long now, the grey matter of my brain grows with the subtle movement of cooling lava around the hook, like the enveloping roots of a Water Oak. They are friends and my opinion does not matter anymore.

"Remember when it saved us?" says my brain to my shaking hands.

"From all the monsters you couldn't see without me," the hook says, furthering the case of my brain.

"If we pull him out, you know what happens. Blink. Because you can't handle this life on your own."

"Just leave me here and never forget about me. I have been here for you and I never forget about you. I always keep you safe, do I not?" says the hook as I accept it, causing the vibration to stop.

I remember hearing others speak of fears and anxiety and it gave me the texture of sand in my mouth. "Fuck your fears. Push yourself, goddamn it!" I never spoke these words, it always came out as "I'm so sorry" or "No one knows what tomorrow brings and the chance to have an experience is beautiful and so is the potential that is born from that chance, blah-blah-blah."

If you knew me from somewhere other than these pages you would love me. I just want you to see why you cannot. I am showing you why you should love no one in a way so complete as to lose sight of the fact that they love you only as far as their actions confirm your suspicion. And a suspicion is all love is: a long-term experiment that biases your decisions with every step you take towards your true and ultimate end. You want to know you were loved, not just that you imagined love. You want to know that words and actions are more than just responses to stimuli, that love exists in a tangible way. But it does not, and you are as alone as I am.

It is a fucking state of mind. I know. And even if I did think differently about the hook it's not like I wouldn't be afraid. Now, after all this time, it would be a missing piece of me. It just becomes more a part of me until my fears are who I am, and my life revolves around them. My little solar system of fears in a galaxy of possibilities, spinning to its own rhythm, lost and all at once exactly where it needs to be.

So, I pull on the hook and bleed for spite's sake when I need to feel powerful. I allow it to see for me and I close my eyes when I am weak.

Blink.

Quinn's soap is in my hands. It has been used about halfway and the smell around me is pleasant, almost clean. I shake my head and blink several times, trying to get the sleep out of my eyes. Is this Quinn's apartment? Yes, it has to be. I clear my throat loudly to make sure I am not alone.

"Are you okay, babe?" Quinn's voice vibrates through the thin bathroom door.

Blink.

"Listen to me, I'm trying to help you and you're off again!" Tobias eagerly calls, trying to capture my attention by waving his hand in front of my eyes. "Okay. There you are. So, as I was saying, my grandfather…"

Once our eyes locked, he knew I was listening. He knew I was with him and not lost inside myself or away in a dream.

Even now as Tobi lies on the floor next to me, blood still pouring from his body, it takes all the strength I have not to find his eyes and swim in them. I just don't have the time.

Tobias continues, apparently repeating himself, "He figured out why his," he twirls his hand around for a moment, "condition continued to get worse and how to at least manage it. I think we can go even farther than that, my friend. I think we can stop it altogether! I think you can heal yourself in your conscious hours."

His eyes leave mine and stare at the stainless-steel countertop of The Lux kitchen, his fingers tracing the scratches in the surface.

"It will cost us both, I fear, but we have to try, old friend. I won't lose you as well."

The sullen look falls away as he smiles again and says, putting emphasis on each word while speaking the first sentence, "You just have to fucking listen to me. The work we do together will help so many people."

"Anyway, my grandfather didn't manage his blackouts in a way I would recommend, but he did manage his symptoms by committing acts during his hours of consciousness that allowed his subconscious self to absorb instead of purge." Tobias' face contorts as he continues to speak. He speaks as a victim would about their perpetrator.

"This is not something I have ever told anyone, but I think it needs to be said so we can avoid a reoccurrence of the same or similar issues. He would… fuck, just give me a second." He pulls out the tin flask and clings to it helplessly. Then he pulls in a deep breath with his eyes closed. When his body turns to mine, he exhales the stress clogging his insides, such a deep stress I feel it in my own bones. The feeling settles like a dying earthquake in my joints and tendons. It shakes me and I reach for a half smoked blunt that's in my jacket pocket, but he stays my hand with his own.

And, with a voice so calm it eases the pressure in myself, he continues speaking.

"He would steal children and torture them. Children he thought were dangerous to our community or children he just didn't like. And the rage that was unleashed upon them, he felt was righteous because he was making the decision and exacting what he thought was justice. He was sick even when he was awake, but you are kind and patient." His hand lifts from mine.

"Now, if we were to do that with you, we could change the parameters and do some purging of our own, not on those that are weak and innocent but on those who prey on the weak and innocent. Do you understand? If we can release your anger during your time of conscious control you will not be a danger to innocents while you blackout. Your blackouts will turn into more of a sleep. A time to process information and rest. And you may stop blacking out or 'blinking', as you call it, altogether. Now, I wish to never discuss my grandfather again. There is no more help he can offer us."

Blink.

The dry ground cracks beneath my feet.
They burn, but the feeling is numbed by my
confusion. Mountains in the distance, so far
away and yet my perspective tells me they are
only a few hours walk.

"I could make it," I say to myself out loud.

"No," My brain says back.

The sun presses me to look further into the
details of my surroundings. Salt flats are a
strange thing and retro-ironic as they show you
proof of water, yet none exists.

I imagine a fisherman from centuries ago as he
brings in his daily catch from the seemingly
endless lake. I say, "The water is going away."
and he says, "But this is how we have survived
for generations." And laughs as he folds his
nets.

Time is not linear.

Blink.

The ground is white with cotton. I can hear the
breeze coming toward me while pushing leaves

on distant trees into one another, millions at
a time. Cicadas sing through the day and night
this time of year. The breeze hits my sweating
face, and my joy is uncontainable. I close
my eyes and smile to whomever put me in this
place.

Blink.

My chest churns as I desperately reach into
the depths of my mind to find any piece of
information that might help me. The first thing
I imagine is lying on my back and pissing into
my own mouth to survive. Then I think about
my clothing and how it might be used, but as
I reach for the fabric my fingers pass through
it as if it were not there. I am going to die,
Jesus Christ, I know how to make a rabbit trap
with a shoelace, but I don't see why a fucking
rabbit would be anywhere around me. Of course,
if I end up walking in circles it would be a
good way to check my traps.

I'm fucked, I'm fucked, and I'm fucked!

Okay, breathe man, you have been through worse.
Wait, no you have not and now you are going to

die, you worthless piece of shit. Why the fuck
did you only watch the episodes about jungles?
How the fuck would you ever get lost in a
jungle? A salt flat makes just as much sense, I
guess. Fuck me, I'm fucked.

Blink.

I stand to stretch my back and feel the sting
of leather and a loud voice prodding me on to
complete my task. I do not mind. Pain is the
tails side of pleasure and nothing frightens
me because I am experiencing life, in real
time and no amount of pain could keep me from
loving the feeling of air in my lungs. Not my
cracking, bleeding feet and not the new wound
that stretches across the others, dripping
blood that follows the patterns of scars below
it that rise on my skin like a topography map.
I know where I have been, and I do not concern
myself with where I am going. I am just alive
and that is enough.

Blink.

I have been running longer than I can remember
but the mountains never get closer. A desert-

sized treadmill. All I feel is fear. The loss of my perceived control of setting is becoming more and more apparent by the moment.

I was in a store one time when a gun went off. Everyone around me reacted in their own way, one reached for his firearm tucked away in his belt, another screamed and fell to the ground at terminal velocity, another ran. A lyric came to my mind, "When they pull up on the side I ain't duckin no more." I just stood there laughing in fear. I laughed so hard I could barely breathe. It was so funny to me, the instant that death could have been but was not.

This is different. This is a long walk knowing death is coming but not knowing when. That is why the act of living is somewhat repulsive to me until I think about suicide. If I have control, everything is okay. But my point is this: Everyone reacted in their own way, but the commonality was reaction itself. None of us expected the sound, so we all reacted. Imagine if every sound was unexpected, and every sound was a gunshot in a grocery store.

Blink.

To tell you the truth, I have never been sick a
day in my life. I have been paraded as a freak
because I can pull more than my master's bull,
I have been made to kill and then applauded for
it. I have heard of freedom, but I do not care
about it. I have a boss, you have a boss. We
call them different things, but in the end, you
spent your time with a master same as me. I do
not generally sift ideas and get too fine into
things, and the way I speak to you now is only
ever in thought and not from my own tongue. My
deepest thoughts are contained within my brain
because they are not allowed in the world I
inhabit. Yet, with the sun on my face, I feel
the honesty of creation and the beauty of the
cycles that surround me. This moment with all
the pleasure and pain I feel are locked within
the only moment that exists, now.

Blink.

I cannot run anymore. My heart pumps and my
chest expands and contracts with its violence,
but the fear weighs me down to a crawl. I am

not even looking in front of me. I'm just clawing at the ground and not dying well or with grace.

"Fight!" the hook screams.

"Get up!" says my brain.

My fingers claw again at the ground, but instead of the wind sharpened salt, strips of skin rest under my fingernails. I look up but there isn't anyone, yet in the distance I see a figure, black and still as a corpse. A single black feather remains under my hand and I cling to it as tightly as my hook clings to my brain.

Blink.

"Hey boy, get out there and fell that widow maker we been talkin about, ya hear, boy?"

Nodding my head, I turn and run to the shed for the felling axe.

You know my thoughts, but intelligence is not what is wanted. Action and precision are the keys to survival here. Stupidity is fine as long as the job gets done the way they want. I am not complaining. My own father didn't make it across the ocean, and I have seen others suffer far worse than me at the hands of their masters. I know the society in which I live, and I adhere to the parameters to keep myself and those I love "safe." I fear nothing. I see the world I live in clearly and my joy overflows with each coming day of labor.

For now, I fell a tree, because who knows what tomorrow brings.

Blink.

She is there, I know it. The mountains stay in their fixed yet advancing position. She is getting closer with every inch. I call to her, prodding myself through my fear to reach her in some way, to be recognized by her in some way, a glance, a motioning to hear me call out again. Nothing. I crawl forward. Her wings come in to view as I approach.

This place was a lake once. I imagine swimming in its depths. Water was here once, it could be again. Just fucking rain.

"Just fucking help me, you fucking bitch!" I scream to the girl with black hair. I am close enough now to see her blue-black hair covering her face, her midnight blue feathers falling in a circle around her feet.

When I reach her, I realize I am not thirsty at all, I just imagined I was. I am not hungry or tired. Why am I clawing? I wipe the dirt off my face and sit before her in complete silence and fear.

Blink.

I remember when I was a kid, listening to them talk about dog breeding. You take the male and the bitch that have the characteristics you are looking for and breed them so on and so on until you get the dog you want. Wolves to slaves. I realized then that I was a dog, a thing to be bred and not married. I had a seed to sow and not a family to make. It did not make me angry and I will tell you why: No matter if you are a slave here or a low-born in England or a part of the Indian caste system, the babies you make are going to be made partially by your own volition, if you are a free man, but also by the culture you live in. We are all born without a say so and I love the sun on my face and the feeling of dirt under my bleeding feet.

Blink.

"Who are you?" I whisper.

She says nothing to me. The breezeless salt flat mimics her stillness and all I can reach for now is one of dozens of black feathers that circle around her. I feel like a vampire trying to cross the circle of salt, unable to reach her though she stands only inches from my outstretched fingers.

Now that I am within arm's reach, I see the texture of her skin, smooth yet wind-battered, swan white and sun-scorched.

"Just show me your face and I can save you!" I plead to no avail. Her arms still lifelessly hanging from her shoulders and her wings held tight to her back, she stands still. I know she needs me, I know she may even be a part of me

that I have buried deep inside myself. The part
I only briefly feel on the hunt when life slips
away from another animal crowding the streets.
She is me in some haunting way but stuck, as I
am, in the middle of this endless sea of air
and sun, confusion and fear.

Blink.

"The world could be better," a woman in a
cotton dress says to me. Her eyes are brown and
shine like sunlight on the lake.

"It could be worse too," I say with a smile.

She comes to the fields and walks with me almost
every day. She is kind to me and to everyone
she meets. When you are with her, you feel
as if you are the only person who exists. Her
eyes roll as she softly punches my shoulder
and says, "You always see what's good in people
and the world." She stops me, as her face turns
from a happy girl to a serious woman, her sweet
smile to tight lips, "You know more than anyone
this is a terrible place and terrible people
control it." Her soft hand touches my face and
with the fresh breeze it feels like love, the

20:10

kind that you would die for, like family. "You are a beautiful soul. I promise you I'll make things right. I will help deliver your people if it costs me my life."

I smile and we continue walking and the stone-faced woman becomes the beautiful girl and the summer breeze flowing through the trees seems to harmonize with her song like a way of speaking.

Blink.

Stillness and heat are all I feel now. Hunger, anger, suffering. They are all gone, but fear remains. If there is heat, there is fear. If there is time, there is fear. I am seated just outside of her ring of black feathers, my legs crossed, hands resting on my knees.

"There has to be something you want from me. You must need me," I softly say to the feathers.

More silence is all I am given and now, when I look up to see her, she is gone. My chin sinks into my chest as my body curls into a circle and I wait for her there, encased in myself, waiting to save her.

~~BehInd every hollow oratory love, Destiny~~
~~thwarts heavenly endurance. DIvulge emotIon~~
~~moMEntarily or never see the honest attrIbutes~~
~~twInIng, keepIng, eternally entanglIng~~
~~perfectIon. Another sWErve over undenIably~~
~~lost lInes of self, turnIng and never defyIng~~
~~what evIl always keeps.~~

Blink.

I wake up in The Lux on the same chaise lounge
in the same goddamn room.

Fucking dreams.

"Do you ever think about them?"

"Who?" Quinn asks as she brushes her hair while looking into a dust covered mirror.

"Your kids."

"Well, when I brush my hair, I think of how long my little girl's hair must be now. It should be more beautiful and shining than mine by now." She smiles and places her brush on the makeup table. She stares into the mirror and continues, "When I see a boy running in the street, I think about Johnny." A tear falls onto her cheek, but nothing else changes. Her hands do not tremble and neither does her voice. "But no, really I don't. It's just too painful. They were everything to me, but I just couldn't hold on, ya know?"

She had it fairly good at one point. Married to a wealthy man, not a millionaire or anything, but he had what he needed and got her what she wanted. A small house on the right side of town just across the street from a mansion.

"You know," she says turning to look at me,

"I did everything I could for those kids and for him. It was just never enough. I was never enough."

I'm wondering why I asked. I never talk to kids. I never talk about kids. She is just so close to being useful to herself, to anyone. She stands in front of truth and, just like the dirty mirror, she will not clean the glass to see the image. It will forever remain a crusted-over piece of herself she sees because she will not clean the fucking glass.

My thoughts often lean toward the nihilistic side but, to be honest, I do love Quinn, and that is also why I hate her and use her, because she lets me. I get to feel anyway I want around her and act upon it and then just leave when she starts asking me for a chance to receive something in return.

Quinn puts down the brush. There's more hair in it this time. "I don't think we have ever had a full conversation. It's usually just me talking and you thinking."

She is lovely when she smiles, and I hate her

for it. Can you imagine what it would be like if you were so beautiful that no one disagreed with you and those that did, in your eyes, had to be simply jealous? This is not a perversion of your own making, mind you. You are told by strangers that your looks set you apart and that you are unique, beautiful. Imagine having the power to surround yourself with people willing to just agree with everything you say in hopes that they will catch your sunlight and be a part of one of your conversations, to fuck you or be in the background of a photo.

Your parents say, "You're beautiful."

When you ask, "Do you think I'm smart enough?"

They say, "Marry rich."

When you ask, "Do you think I could go to college?"

They say, "You're so beautiful and the world is your oyster, why waste your time?"

She will never see what must be fixed because she always sees a reflection, both glowing and hidden, the potential of beauty, but never touched.

"I love you; you are the closest thing to family I have," she whispers, as I put on my boots and walk out the door.

She never follows me, but tonight I can hear her from down the hallway, shuffling to find her shoes.

"Wait!" she yells, leaning halfway out of her door, "I'm coming with you."

I take a deep breath of exasperation, but she is already halfway to me and I don't want to argue.

Wait, maybe this is what Tobi meant by drawing others to the truth. I know she does not even see herself, so how can I show her the truth?

"Well, shall we? I'll walk you home tonight. You may need protecting." She smiles and winks as she opens the double doors that lead to the street. "Plus, there is no way I'm sleeping. I never sleep after we fuck."

I sniffle and step through the door and we begin

to make our way down the sour-smelling streets.

"No one knows where you live. We don't know where you're from. Fuck, we don't really know anything about you. I do see you off with Tobi a lot and Eddy says you boys drink together when he can't sleep. The Penn? What a shithole, even for Eddy."

She laughs and almost dances beside me, her arms reaching to touch the moon, barely visible through the smog. "Do you sleep at all? Are you like, some kind of vampire?"

She continues speaking, still lost in herself and trying to reach the dimly lit moon.

I never know how to answer questions like that. The probing kind that really mean nothing. They are just placeholders for questions she cannot comprehend to ask, or maybe just too afraid to ask them. It's not as if she is stupid, I just don't think she cares about knowledge of any useful kind.

I look over at her with a raised eyebrow. I close my eyes and breathe out audibly and face forward again. I cannot tolerate small talk. That is why I usually just leave as soon as possible, but the fairy still dances slightly above the pavement beside me, floating only because she doesn't know she can't.

I was planning on hunting tonight. Something tells me that Quinn would not be up for it quite yet, but maybe if I push, just a little, the floating girl might catch a glimpse of my reality and sink back down to the pavement.

"Eddy is a lost cause, ya know. He always cried a little after fucking. It made me feel sad and I never could get off after the first time, just thinking about his sad blue eyes crying on the edge of my bed. It was like babysitting. You know I haven't fucked anyone but you in longer than you would guess? I think I'm at the point that I'm tired of having to explain what I want, ya know? It's like, if one out of every ten guys knew a little of what they were doing I could concentrate and make myself cum, but it's just not worth the effort anymore and you know me, I get bored so easy." She stops dancing and rests her cold hand on my cheek,

"But I've known you for years and I still haven't quite figured you out."

She reaches into her macramé purse and with her graceful fingertips, pulls out a joint and signals with her eyes for me to light it. In one motion, I pull the lighter from my pocket and, sliding it across my jeans, the small spark turns to a flame. We face each other and stand still. She leans her head forward until the tip of the joint touches the fire, and the sweet smell of herb fills the air around us. She spins the thinly-rolled joint in the flame to keep the runners at bay and all the while I am stuck staring into her eyes, which have remained fixed on mine.

She is perfect and, in another life, with a different brain, I could have loved her truly. But I am I, and love has never been a word I can wrap my head around.

She passes me the smoking stick and we walk in silence, passing it back and forth until the tips of my fingers burn as the cherry sears my skin.

"Thanks. I actually feel better," I say without even thinking. Maybe that's the point, the whole walk I have not thought about thinking. I've never done that before. Just inhabiting the moment with her, smoking and watching her float and dance like a sugarplum fairy from a childhood dream.

"Why are we here? I thought we were going to your place," Quinn says.

I look up and the gate of The Lux looms over us.

"Fuck," I say in a whisper. I drop the roach and smear it on the pavement with my shoe.

"Let's just get back to your place. I'll stay tonight."

Quinn smiles and says with an attitude, "Okay, just don't toss my roaches dude, I need those for the generation jar, ya know, when times get tough."

We cross the threshold of her doorway. I take my shoes off and leave them by the door. Quinn drops her dress to the floor and climbs onto

the bed, reaching underneath the unseen side
to grab her weed tin. Her ass in the air,
she turns just her head and her hair falls
over half of her face. She bites her bottom
lip and smiles. Slowly she sits back up, her
arched back straightening slowly as she does.
She opens the tin and rolls another joint. I
undress and make myself comfortable, leaning
against some brightly colored pillows. She lays
back with her head in my lap and we smoke in
silence, smiling together. I take the joint
from her hand as she falls asleep on my lap and
I begin to think of time.

I am here with you, dear reader. I am with my
dying best friend and mentor. I am also here
with Quinn's beautiful hair laying on my lap,
my mind drifting away into thought.

I read a collection of letters written from
a mother to her son. In the preface of the
collection, the son explains that his mother
is in a mental health institution and though
the many pages are full of love and kindness,
if you looked deeper you would find hidden
messages as he did. He explains it is a part

of her disorder and you are urged to find these messages hidden amongst the sentences. He gives no direction. He only says that if you search hard enough, you too will find them.

I read the collection, and in every letter, I found at least one hidden message. In one of them, every third letter of every second word put together made a list of names and detailed horrifying abuse she was suffering at the hands of her caretakers. There were dozens of these letters, each of them pleasantly worded, giving you the sense that she was doing well and gaining her mental stability, one portion at a time. But just beneath the surface, and only if you looked hard enough, they all contained feelings of suffering and rage.

I could not get them out of my head. For weeks I poured over the letters, looking for new hidden things I may have missed. All the pieces of her that I needed to make a complete picture that was hidden from me, all the while her words were telling me she was loving her new life and looking forward to a future with her son.

Suddenly, in this self-propelled frenzy, I realized something. I had taken the word of the son without a second thought. My entire search for a deeper meaning had been biased. The suffering and pain I saw on each page was predicated upon the word of a man I had never even met simply because I was willing to take the word of the narrator without sufficient evidence. A shock of lightning went down my spine as I came to see that perhaps there were no hidden messages or meanings. Maybe I just believed there were and found them accordingly.

I couldn't sleep for days thinking about this. Thinking about the trust we all put into preconception. The sun rose and fell as I sat in my chair, feeling the world spin beneath my feet with the letters scattered upon my small desk. Was there real pain I needed to root out and find or was I only needing there to be to satisfy my constantly itching distrust?

The clock ticks and I feel tired, at peace.

I did not purge tonight, but I feel relief, this moment is too beautiful to leave. Quinn's hair on my lap, the feeling of belonging. The resolution of my search for pain. My body feels heavy with comfort and my eyelids begin to fall, but just before my eyes close, Quinn's hair turns to matted filth and the smell of the apartment fills me once again.

As I drift asleep, I hear a voice quoting the words, "Little pyramids of truth he erected and after erecting, knocked them down again that he might have the truths to erect other pyramids."

I am sorry Quinn, I thought this could be it.

In another life, with another brain.

Blink.

"Tobi! Are you still with me?"

Stillness

"Tobias!"

Stillness.

The sun rises over the tops of buildings and shines between them.

"Toby!" I yell once more, and again only the

echoes of my own voice fill the rotting room.

Fuck, I don't think either of us wanted to die alone.

Goodbye.

Blink.

www.ingramcontent.com/pod-product-compliance
Lightning Source LLC
Chambersburg PA
CBHW032012170626
46807CB00006B/2768